the hour
OF THE MOTH

A
Camilla
Randall
Mystery

ANNE R. ALLEN

Thalia

one

. . .

Open Flame

On a Friday morning in early September, the owner of the coffee house down the street rushed into my bookstore looking as if she'd been the model for Edvard Munch's "The Scream." She tore at her luxurious dark hair as if trying to rid it of invisible bats.

I'd always found her intimidating. Lupe, her name was, Lupe Sorensen. She was a gorgeous ex-showgirl who stood six foot three, radiating the confidence of a woman who'd made her own way in life. But today the confidence was missing.

"The Moth!" Her voice was raspy as she leaned on the counter. "The Moth! I'm going to have to kill the Moth."

Okay, maybe not invisible bats, but moths. Or perhaps one particularly important moth?

She reached across the counter and grabbed my hand. "Camilla, you have to do something. Can you help, hon? We'll have to turn away a full damn house tonight. Morro Bay is packed with tourists this weekend."

I gave her hand a polite, reassuring squeeze before I pulled away. We did indeed have a lot of visitors in our beachy California town right now, drawn by our perfect Indian Summer weather. Some were my customers — who were now giving us disapproving stares.

"I'd love to help, but you'll have to explain. Who is the Moth?"

"Not who. What." A customer's voice piped up from the Science Fiction section. "It's the storytelling show they have at the Otter Café every month. Lupe, don't tell me the show is off for tonight? I've got a great story to tell."

A silver-haired man wearing a Friends of the Library tee shirt emerged and gave Lupe a hug. "Calm down, love. I'm sure Camilla will help."

I was aware there'd been an event at the coffee house on the first Friday evening of the month all summer. Customers parked all over the street, often blocking the driveway to my cottage behind the store.

"So what's the problem with the Moth?" I gave her a sympathetic smile.

"Boyd Ferrell is coming tonight. *The* Boyd Ferrell."

The Friend of the Library turned to me to explain. "Boyd is a rock star in the storytelling world. He's been on NPR."

Lupe beamed with pride.

A lightbulb went on in my head. "Oh, the Moth Radio Hour. I listen to that sometimes. So, what's the problem with Mr. Ferrell? Does he need a ride from the airport or something?"

Lupe looked down at me as if I might not be right in the head.

"No! It's the grease trap, sweetie. It's leaking."

Okay. Grease trap. That sounded pretty awful. I made a sympathetic face, but couldn't think of anything polite to say, since I didn't have a clue what a grease trap was, or what it had to do with a public radio star.

Lupe's voice rose. "It's a grease trap we don't even use. It's left over from the last tenant. They sold fish and chips. The thing was supposed to be capped. But it's leaking all over my damn patio. Stinky slime. The landlord says he'll send somebody to fix it on Tuesday, but meanwhile, my Moth event can't go on."

"So maybe Camilla can host the Moth event here?" Mr. Library Friend gave me a wide smile and put a book he'd been holding on the counter. "Don't you have a courtyard out back?"

Lupe nodded like mad.

Oh, dear. This wasn't going to be fun for me, but I could see good manners required me to do what I could. I'd never seen Lupe so stressed. I gave her a reassuring smile as I sorted my thoughts.

Unfortunately, the courtyard was my buffer between my work life and my "me" life — the barrier that separated my little cottage from the store. It was also the territory of my cat Buckingham, who would be seriously put out. And it sounded like a whole lot of work. Event planning had never been my forte. That had always been the territory of my late mother, the countess. But I stifled my selfish thoughts.

"Of course you may use my courtyard." I nodded at the Library Friend, whose name was Don or Dan as I remembered, and gave Lupe's hand another squeeze. "But I don't have any chairs or a microphone or anything."

"We'll take care of everything. We'll even bring the fire pit." Lupe grinned. "Your place will be perfect. I'll put a big sign on my door pointing people here."

She ran out the door with considerably more cheer than when she'd arrived. Dan the Library Friend followed close behind her, leaving the book he'd almost bought on the counter. I wondered if he had a crush on Lupe. He was a recent widower, as I remembered.

A few minutes later, a parade of the café's wait staff came in, carrying folding chairs. I directed them to the driveway that led to the courtyard.

My phone beeped and I grabbed it from my purse.

"Camilla, what the hell is going on?"

Oh, dear. It was Ronzo — my boyfriend, whose band had played until 2 AM last night. He was back in the cottage trying to "catch some z's" as he put it.

"I'm so sorry. It's the Moth. They have to move it here because of a leaky grease trap, whatever that is."

"A moth. You've got an entire battalion of chair-carriers invading our courtyard because of a moth?"

"Well, it's really because of Boyd Ferrell. Apparently he's going to be in Morro Bay tonight to tell a story, and he's famous."

"Boyd effing Ferrell? You're inviting Boyd Ferrell into our home?"

"You know Boyd Ferrell?" I found it ominous when Ronzo called it "our" home. I loved him to pieces, but I'd been trying to steer him toward getting his own place ever since he moved out here from New Jersey in July.

"Every musician in Jersey knows about Boyd. Session bass player who sometimes recorded with Bon Jovi. Mostly he was the bouncer from Hell at a club in Atlantic City. Put people in the hospital every weekend and nearly killed his girlfriend, who was Richie Sambora's ex. Did some time for it. Not a nice guy."

Ronzo's anger gave me a chill. It wasn't like him.

"Oh, it can't be the same man. This one is on public radio." Of course, if it was the same person, this was distressing news for all of us. My shoulders tensed. What had I done? I watched two of Lupe's employees carrying a large, round firepit toward my driveway. A firepit. An open flame. Was that safe in the middle of a drought? It was probably too late for me to change my mind.

Ronzo gave a rough laugh. "Could be, or maybe Boyd has slowed down some. He'd be in his fifties."

Ronzo was trying to alleviate my anxiety, but these days, he tended to push me into worry mode. Living together in my tiny former motel cottage wasn't turning out to be a great experiment. Now that he'd formed a band with his friend Joe Torres, he was out late nearly every night, and I had a strict schedule, with a store to run.

"It's only for one night," I said finally. "Just a few hours — from seven-thirty to ten. You'll be playing at Fisherman Jack's, so you won't even see him. I don't think there will be much time for Mr. Ferrell to beat up any of our Friends of the Library, or strangle the NPR fans with their tote bags." I tried to laugh.

"Let's hope so." Ronzo spoke in a flat voice. "I sincerely hope so. He'd better be gone by the time I get home."

two

. . .

The Mists of Avalon

he evening started pretty well. Lupe's people brought a folding table where she set up a coffee maker, a cooler full of soda, and assorted baked goods, which people seemed to be buying up fast. I usually close up my store at six, but I stayed open another hour, and was able to make a few sales as the audience came through on their way to the courtyard. After that, they'd have to come down the driveway.

Ronzo had suggested I stay open during the performance, to make more sales as people went home after the event. But I told him it would be too long a day for me. What I didn't tell him was I very much wanted to hear Boyd Ferrell's stories, and maybe find out why Ronzo hated him so much — and why Lupe was so giddy about his visit.

At seven, I closed the store and ventured into the courtyard. People had already claimed most of the folding chairs, and the first row was full. The front row people seemed to know each other.

I joined Lupe and her crew behind the food-vending table. Lots of customers stood in line, but she didn't look happy.

"Are those your storytellers in the front row?"

She nodded as she handed a customer a carrot muffin and a cup for coffee.

"Most of them. But Boyd Ferrell isn't here. I'm going nuts here. I hope he can find us." She looked down the driveway to the street and gave a quick gasp.

"There he is. Looking just the same, the bastard…"

I would have known it was the infamous Mr. Ferrell even without her reaction. He sauntered into the courtyard as if he owned it, wearing a blue satin coach's jacket dotted with silver stars and a matching ball cap. He had long, dark, rock-star hair, some serious muscles, and a gleaming, practiced smile.

"Hi there, Lupe." He gave her a bear hug.

She flushed. The woman obviously had a serious crush — or maybe more than that. She and Boyd must have had some history together.

Lupe's crew seemed smitten too. Two women fawned over him, offering him free treats.

"He hasn't aged a bit." Lupe beamed at me as Boyd glad-handed his fans waiting in the food line. "Even though it's been over ten damn years." Her cheeks were still pink. "I didn't know if he'd even remember me."

"Do you know him from when you were performing in Las Vegas?" I didn't want to pry, but it would be good to know.

"Atlantic City. I did some shows there in the late '90s. Did you know he sometimes sat in with Bon Jovi? Stole Richie Sambora's girlfriend."

Okay, this guy was certainly Ronzo's bouncer from Hell.

The crowd swelled quickly and was getting bigger than I'd pictured — well over fifty people. As they streamed in, I could see it would be standing room only. Overwhelming. I would have liked to buy one of Lupe's famous carrot muffins, but the line was too long. I pushed my way through the crowd to my cottage and found Buckingham cowering under the bed, poor thing.

After I fed him, I spread a piece of stale bread with almond butter and heated up the dregs of my morning coffee. Then I sat on my front step with my meagre dinner, avoiding the crowd-crush around the fire pit. September tends to be warm here, but the nights were getting chilly.

Lupe showed off her show business background when she took the mic and gave a polished introduction of the storytellers. There were to be ten, including Boyd Ferrell, who was seated in the front row with a couple of his fans who sat cross-legged on the cold bricks in front of him. Dan Fiedler, the Library Friend, was on the list too. He'd waved at me when he came in.

According to Moth storytelling rules, each tale had to be true, and based on the storyteller's own experiences. The theme was "Did That Really Happen?"

The first was one of Lupe's employees — Felicity Grant — a lumpy, twenty-something woman with a whiny voice and unfortunate hair. She told a wild tale of living on the streets of San Francisco at the age of ten, abandoned by her feckless hippie parents, befriended by the ghost of Michael Jackson. She had us on the verge of tears.

A silver haired gentleman wearing a skipper's hat told a "fish that got away" saga in a deep southern drawl that got everybody laughing.

But the funniest was Dan the Library Friend's story about swimming far out into the bay after partaking of an edible, and having a long, cathartic conversation about life and death with a surfer in a wetsuit whose only response was a loud bark — because he was actually a harbor seal.

He was followed by Irene DeSoto, a local Tarot reader who had been urging me to carry more New Age items. Ronzo had been saying the same thing because he wanted to start offering Tarot readings again. Irene wore a flowing dress and shawl, with her gray hair pulled into a long braid. She launched into a spooky tale of meeting what she was sure was an actual elf in the nearby "Elfin Forest" who warned her of a dangerous man with a head full of stars. She punctuated each scene with the chant, "the star man will die." People made "woo-woo" sounds as she chanted.

Everybody clapped wildly when Boyd took the mic at the end of the first set. He told a hilarious story about meeting the Rolling Stones in Atlantic City, with the usual Keith Richards jokes. His delivery was polished, but a little canned, as if he'd told the story every night for years. But he didn't seem like the dangerous man Ronzo had described. Maybe prison had mellowed him.

There was an intermission so everybody could buy more drinks and pastries. A couple of people asked me to open the store, but I wasn't feeling up to it and urged them to come back in the morning.

"You doing okay?" Lupe re-emerged from the crowd and gave me a smile. She had a well-dressed Black man in tow she introduced as Cassius Burgh. I'd seen him at the beginning of the storytelling, hovering around Boyd. He looked out of place in a bespoke suit and Italian shoes.

I stood and offered them a seat on my step, but they declined. Mr. Burgh asked me about Ronzo, so I explained he was down the street playing at Fisherman Jack's. He seemed much more interested in Ronzo's music than the storytelling and said a polite goodbye as he eagerly took off toward Jack's. I wondered how he knew Ronzo, who didn't spend a lot of time with men in suits. But Ronzo had been a music reviewer for *Rolling Stone* at one point. Maybe Mr. Burgh was an agent or something.

The second half of the evening brought some spookier tales. One man claimed to have met Bigfoot on a hike at Big Sur. An overly-made-up woman named Alice told a story of how her ex-husband tried to get her to give him the house in the divorce by making her think the place was haunted. She almost believed him because she was "very spiritual." But it turned out he'd been trapping raccoons and letting them loose in her attic.

I was getting tired toward the end, but for the finale, Boyd launched into a truly frightening classic ghost story that woke me right up. He called it his "Mists of Avalon" story. It was half *Flying Dutchman* and half Hitchcock's *Rear Window*. He told how he'd been sailing off Catalina last summer when a thick mist descended, and he got disoriented. But he was sure he witnessed a man dropping a woman's body overboard from a yacht not far from Avalon harbor. The next day the yacht was gone. To this day, he didn't know if he had seen a real murder or not.

There was a standing ovation — although of course most people had been standing anyway. Lupe thanked Boyd a little too warmly.

Then she opened up the mic to anyone who wanted to tell a story. A dozen or more eager people raised their hands.

Oh, dear. I hadn't been prepared for this. How long was it going to last? I looked at my watch. It was already nearly ten. Some of the crowd dispersed, but about half stayed, many of them swarming around Boyd.

Damn. I was in for a long night.

three

. . .

Falling off a Train of Thought

Felicity was still selling food. At least there wasn't a long line.

I asked for a carrot muffin, but she said all she had left was bran or pineapple-coconut. And the coffee maker was empty.

"I loved your story." I smiled as I accepted a bran muffin. "But what a horrible thing to go through at such a young age. Did you ever find your parents?"

"I found my mom, but she died of an overdose a year later." Felicity spoke in a flat tone, as if she were talking about the weather.

"And your dad? Did you find him?"

"Oh, yeah. I know where my dad is." Her voice darkened. "I wish he'd been the one who died."

Okay. Not the cheeriest of conversationalists. Alice the raccoon lady pushed past me and gave a huge sigh. Her lavish eye make-up was beginning to smudge above her cheeks, so she looked a bit like a raccoon herself. I worked at keeping a straight face.

"No carrot muffins?" Raccoon Alice was in high dudgeon. "But that Boyd Ferrell guy had about six of them. You couldn't save some for paying customers?"

Felicity looked as if she might burst into tears. Luckily a young man appeared with more coffee and some cookies.

I escaped to my cottage step to eat my bran muffin. Alice wasn't a bad person — she'd offered me a great deal on Tarot decks and crystals she used to sell at craft fairs — but she seemed to have a temper when somebody came between her and her muffins.

Most of the open mic. storytelling was pretty amateurish — what somebody called "old men falling off their train of thought" — but a number were fairly compelling.

Not everybody was compelled, though. Boyd had moved to the back row, where a circle of fans surrounded him, peppering him with questions in stage whispers that must have infuriated the amateur storytellers. Even worse, Raccoon Alice pushed through the crowd and tried to grab one of Boyd's muffins, which sat on a chair beside him. He slapped her hand away. She hissed the word "asshole" at him so loud the storyteller stopped mid-sentence.

Unfortunately, Lupe seemed to have disappeared. I hoped she'd put an end to the program soon. If she didn't, I would. I needed some peace and quiet and it was nearly my bedtime.

Of course, that was when Ronzo showed up. He looked even crankier than I felt.

"Sorry. I thought this thing would be over by ten." I stood and gave him a hug. "Fisherman Jack's can't be closing now — is your band on a break?"

He nodded and looked over at Boyd, now holding court in the back row, almost out of hearing of the other storytellers. Felicity stood behind him, eating a snickerdoodle. She looked less enchanted than the rest of Boyd's fans. But then, she seemed to have a resting disgruntled face.

"That creep looks exactly the same. And he's still got ladies hanging all over him. They'll regret it." Ronzo's body stiffened with anger. He was usually a relaxed, easy-going man. He also didn't usually come home in the middle of a gig. This couldn't be only because of Richie Sambora's ex. Something very personal must have happened with Boyd and Ronzo back in New Jersey.

Boyd looked over at us and seemed to recognize Ronzo. He smiled and waved. Ronzo waved back, but he didn't even fake a smile.

"I guess I have to say hello now he's recognized me. Then I've got to get back. It's only a fifteen-minute break, but I wanted to make sure things were going okay. I hope these people are gonna split pretty soon. I know how much you need your sleep."

He gave my shoulder a squeeze before venturing back into the crowd. He headed straight for Boyd. I did not want to watch this, but I could hear Ronzo saying something to Boyd, who replied with anger, jumped up, and looked as if he might start a physical fight.

Lupe saw this was the moment to close the show, thank goodness. She took the mic and thanked everybody for coming. Ronzo waved at me and took off running down the driveway. Finally, people started to disperse. All except the Boyd Ferrell fan club. They closed in around him, regaling him their own storytelling hopes and dreams as he sat in bored-looking silence. He was probably one of those narcissists who was only interested in conversation when he was doing all the talking himself.

I hoped Ronzo would explain their unpleasant *contretemps* later.

The nautical silver fox lingered with the Boyd crowd, then moved toward my step. He introduced himself as Bernard Lanier and complimented me on the bookstore's display window out on Main Street. His Southern gentleman manners put me at ease.

"Are you the Camilla Randall who used to write the Manners Doctor newspaper columns?"

The question startled me. It had been years since my etiquette column had been dropped by the syndicate, and my Manners Doctor advice books weren't selling well, even in my own store.

"I knew the countess," Mr. Lanier said. "Your mother gave the most elegant parties."

I tried to smile. My mother had acquired her title from a phony Portuguese count who ran through the entire family fortune, and then some.

"My mother enjoyed being a good hostess." I hoped I managed to keep a breezy tone. "I liked your fish story."

Irene the Tarot reader joined us. Her bracelets jingled like a bell on a cat. She grabbed my arm.

"You could at least carry the Rider-Waite deck. And the Golden Dawn. And crystals. We all need crystals. Wasn't Alice going to sell you some of her crystal collection?"

I nodded and attempted a smile. "Yes, Ronzo is helping me put together an order for some New Age items."

"I like crystals," Mr. Lanier gave Irene a warm smile. "I'm so glad you're getting some New Age things. Nobody reads books anymore. They watch Netflix on their phones."

Alas, the two of them were probably right. Ronzo had been giving me the same advice. The store was barely limping along on income from book sales. He was going to start doing Tarot readings in our back storage room, once we got it cleaned out. He'd been taught by his Romany grandmother and his predictions were uncannily good. I wondered how Irene would feel about the competition.

As they delved deep into Tarot talk, I managed to escape and joined Lupe, who was directing her employees as they cleared my courtyard. They were cleverly using a garden wheelbarrow to carry stacks of chairs and other big items back to the coffee shop.

All except the fire pit. Lupe explained it would be too hot to carry, even though the fire was out.

Boyd and his admirers still sat around the cooling pit, looking as if they had no intention of leaving. A man in a black beanie was telling him an endless story about selling frozen yogurt to Keith Richards in L.A., and another kept interrupting with his own tales of meeting rock music royalty. Boyd didn't appear to be encouraging them, but sat still and unsmiling as they went on and on. Obviously nothing was going to stop these people from talking about their one brush with celebrity.

Finally, I told Lupe I needed to get ready for bed. I had to hope she'd make sure her people left things as clean as they'd found them. At least they had removed the microphone and cleared the "stage" area. Only a few of the featured storytellers — plus Boyd and his flock of wannabes — remained, hovering near the cooling firepit.

I went inside, coaxed Buckingham out of his under-bed sanctuary, fed him a couple of treats, and poured myself a brandy.

I was sitting in my easy chair, taking a warming sip from the snifter when I heard the scream.

four

. . .

Expired

It was a woman's scream. High-pitched and sustained. Horror movie-worthy. I put down my brandy, picked up my over-stuffed purse in case I needed a weapon, and ventured out to the courtyard.

There, still sitting in his chair near the firepit, was Boyd Ferrell, looking a bit limp and pale, listing to one side, as if he'd tried to stand up, but decided to take a nap instead. Above him was Lupe, the screamer. And around her, in the shadows, were two of her staff people, plus Bernard Lanier, Dan the Library Friend, Irene and Alice, and four or five members of Boyd's fan club.

"He just fell over." Felicity, the sad muffin girl, ran to me, her face as pale as Boyd's. She seemed the only person in the group capable of moving. "He stopped answering questions, and then we thought he'd passed out or something, and most of the people already left, so Lupe shook his shoulder to tell him it was time to go, but he fell sideways like that. And there's blood. In his hair. It's all dripping down."

There was a small pool of blood on the bricks below Boyd's chair, and streaks of it on his star-spangled jacket.

"911?" I said. "Has anybody called 911?"

They hadn't, so I did. I told the dispatcher there was a person in distress in the courtyard of the bookstore. I figured I shouldn't use the word corpse. It wasn't up to me to declare Boyd dead. I returned to the huddle of people who were still standing around him, mumbling to each other. They hardly moved — as if they were living in a slow-motion video. The only sound was Lupe's sobs.

"The gentleman is dead," Mr. Lanier said in a flat voice. "No point in bothering the paramedics. You just need the coroner."

"How are you sure he's dead?" I had to ask. Had they even checked his pulse?

If it weren't for the blood, I could believe Boyd was in some sort of trance, about to spring out of it like some grotesque Jack-in-the-Box. One more of his stories with a twisty ending.

I took a compact from my make-up bag and put it under his nose, hoping the mirror might show some breathing going on. But it wasn't. Okay. We were definitely dealing with a corpse.

I tried to soothe Lupe, who couldn't stop crying. She took gulps of air after a few more big, hicuppy sobs. One of her crew, a young blond surfer called Skip, held her against his Billabong hoodie as she wept into his shoulder.

I handed her a couple of tissues.

"I still cared for him," she said after she finally caught her breath. "I thought we might pick up where we left off fifteen years ago. I was afraid he wouldn't even remember me, but he did. He wanted to get together…"

More sobs ensued.

I did feel sorry for the woman. But I'd be happier when she and her weepy entourage toddled off home, and my property was corpse-free.

The paramedics came pretty quickly. They were efficient as they packed Boyd's body into the ambulance, but were not willing to speculate what had happened. They said the deceased had expired from "a medical emergency."

A medical emergency like somebody stabbed him? Maybe not. I guess if he'd been stabbed, there would have been more blood. And why didn't he scream? And for goodness' sake, how could it have happened with everybody standing right there with him?

Two police officers showed up shortly after the paramedics and they seemed to think they needed the names and addresses of everybody who was there when the body was discovered. This took a tedious amount of time. Lupe cried softly while Skip and Felicity gave her comforting shoulder pats. The rest of them hovered nearby, sniffling into handkerchiefs, seemingly rooted to the courtyard.

I was still standing by the fire pit when Ronzo showed up.

"Geez, why didn't you phone me? Is it true?" His tone was loud and accusatory — as if I'd been trying to keep something from him. "Everybody over at Jack's is saying somebody killed Boyd Ferrell."

"He's certainly dead, but we don't know exactly how. It's not like anybody saw an attack. And people have been standing around him this whole time." I spoke in a carefully lowered tone, hoping he'd take the hint and be more discreet. "Right now, they're saying Boyd suffered a 'medical emergency' and expired."

"Expired. He expired? Like an effing carton of milk?" Ronzo's tone was much too loud and naturally got the attention of both policemen. "I don't think so. I'll put money on it that somebody speeded along Boyd's expiration date. A lot of people wanted him dead. Look. Isn't that blood on the bricks by the firepit?"

The taller officer — a polite man I'd met before named Dwayne Pilchard —came over to Ronzo and gave him the once-over.

"What are you doing here, sir? The entertainment is over."

"I happen to live here," Ronzo said in his most defiant New Jersey tone. He put a proprietary arm around my shoulders. "My band is playing at the bar down the street, but when I saw the police car, I wanted to find out what's going on and make sure my girlfriend is okay."

Officer Pilchard gave me an inquisitive look. "You okay, Ms. Randall?"

I nodded. "Everything's fine, considering. I'm just tired."

"So you think somebody wanted to kill the deceased?" Officer Pilchard took a confrontational tone with Ronzo. "Do you have anybody in mind?"

I shot Ronzo a warning look, but he ignored it and went full speed ahead.

"Boyd Ferrell was a convicted felon and lowlife scum. I don't believe he turned legit because he was on public radio. The truth is a lot of people hated him. It's a miracle nobody's killed the jerk before now. I find it hard to believe he'd just politely, um, 'expire' at a story-telling evening."

Lupe let out another wail, but Ronzo had Officer Pilchard hooked. The policeman took out his iPad and started taking notes. Lots of notes. This was going to take a while.

I gave Ronzo a quick kiss on the cheek and offered a smile to Officer Pilchard. "I'm exhausted, so I'm going in to get ready for bed. I'm sure you can take care of everything, Ronzo. If anybody needs me, you'll know where I am."

"Sorry, but I have to get back to Fisherman Jack's," Ronzo said. "We've got another set. Leave it to Boyd Ferrell to ruin that too…"

I walked away while he was in mid-rant. Which was dreadfully impolite of me, but I couldn't bear it. Ronzo was drawing attention to himself for no reason. He hadn't needed to say one word to the police about his dislike of Mr. Ferrell.

I escaped into my cottage — as annoyed with Ronzo as I was with the rest of them. Yes, maybe Boyd had been lowlife scum. Maybe he had been the love of Lupe's life. Or maybe he'd simply been an egotistical storyteller. I didn't care. All I wanted was quiet. And to be alone. If I didn't get some alone time, I might expire somebody myself.

five

. . .

Star Man

I had just picked up my brandy again, and Buckingham was happily purring on my lap when there was a faint knock on my front door. I almost didn't hear it — a little tap. Then another. Way too quiet for the police. And Ronzo wouldn't knock. This was his home, after all, whether I liked it or not.

"Are you in there, dear?" said a soft woman's voice. Irene, the Tarot reader.

I invited her in and motioned for her to join me in the living room, which was only polite. Unfortunately, I really wasn't in the mood for a visit. My Manners Doctor self would have told me to offer her a brandy, but I didn't.

"His death was foretold." Irene settled her voluminous dress, shawls, and scarves into my couch. "He was the star man. Like the elf in the Elfin Forest predicted. 'The star man must die.' That's what the elf said. Didn't you see his hat?"

"The elf, um, had a hat?" I was not going to enjoy this conversation. I wondered if maybe poor Irene had a touch of dementia.

She scoffed at me. "No, silly. Boyd Ferrell. He was wearing a cap with stars on it. There were stars on his jacket too. Do you know what the Star card means?"

I shook my head. "I'm afraid I don't. It's my boyfriend Ronzo who's the expert on Tarot. But it was quite the eye-catching ensemble Boyd was wearing." I took a sip of brandy and managed to smile. I hoped Irene was going to start making sense soon.

"It's the happy card. Hope, renewal, creativity. So at first I thought it was auspicious that he was wearing that hat. But now I know he was the man with the head full of stars that the elf warned me about."

"So you think Boyd was killed by an elf?" I tried to sound sympathetic, but my tolerance for delusional nonsense was waning fast. Buckingham sensed my impatience and jumped off my lap.

"Of course not." Irene flipped her long gray braid over her shoulder. "The elf wasn't of this realm. I saw him on the astral plane. But Boyd was real, and all those people were swarming around him. Some of them were angry. You know, because they all want to get on NPR, and they didn't think it was fair he got on the Moth Hour, they didn't, because of him being a felon and all that."

"I did hear that Boyd had been in prison for assaulting his girlfriend. I'm sure the people on NPR thought he'd been rehabilitated." So other people had shared Ronzo's negative opinion of Mr. Ferrell. At least Ronzo had been right about Boyd's large collection of enemies.

"And I suppose that boyfriend of yours told you that? The guy who looks like Jon Bon Jovi and sounds like Tony Soprano?"

I had to smile. "He does look a bit like a younger Jon Bon Jovi with his hair long like that, doesn't he?"

"Well, I'd be careful, honey. I think your boyfriend killed the star man. I heard him threaten Boyd less than an hour before Boyd suddenly got dead." She gave me an odd, penetrating look. "That's why I'm here, Camilla. To warn you. Your guy is dangerous. He's only been here, what? Three months? He may be sweet as pie to you now, but when he gets mad, he's going to get crazier and crazier. That's how all the abusers are. You should watch some Lifetime movies."

Now I'd had enough. I stood and gave Irene a stiff smile.

"Thank you so much for thinking of me, Irene, but I've known Ronson Zolek for many years and he's a kind and gentle man. He's not capable of hurting me, or Boyd Ferrell, or anybody else. The paramedics told me Boyd died of what they call 'a medical emergency'—

you know, like a stroke. Maybe something in his head burst and caused the bleeding from his ears or something. The blood was mostly in his hair, from what I could see. Now I'm afraid I must get to bed. I'm exhausted."

Irene didn't pick up on my cue.

"It could have been poison," she said in a matter-of-fact tone. "Maybe something injected with a needle — like pentobarbital, the stuff they use to put down a sick pet. The people around him could have been using. They looked pretty scruffy, some of them. They'd know how to inject somebody. You sure your Bon Jovi boy isn't on some kind of drugs? He hangs out with those homeless guys."

Yes, Ronzo's band was made up of several formerly unhoused musicians. Not exactly something to condemn him for.

There was another knock on the door. More assertive this time. I stood between my chair and the door and took a deep breath, trying not to let out the scream that was threatening to escape.

"Irene?" said a man's voice. "Is Irene in there?"

"I'm here, Bernard." She called over her shoulder in the direction of the door, only moving her neck, as if her body were glued to my couch.

Bernard Lanier burst in, captain's cap askew. "Irene darlin' we must go. The tide is going out and my dinghy will be stranded. We'll have no way of getting out to the *Mary Sue*."

So. Irene and Bernard seemed to be living together on his yacht. Interesting. He hadn't been moored here more than a month or so, as far as I knew. Irene used to live alone in an apartment over the surf shop down the street. She used to give her Tarot readings in the back room behind the surfboards.

"Thanks so much for taking Irene home," I said with another fake smile. "I'm afraid I'm about to collapse. It's been a stressful night."

"It has indeed." Bernard gave me an understanding nod and helped Irene up from the couch. He seemed like a nice enough man. But I was not unhappy to see them go. What had Irene been talking about? Poison injections? Predicted by elves? She must watch a lot of those Lifetime movies.

My cell phone rang in my pocket. I picked up, but I really was ready for this evening to end. I'm afraid my "hello" was not altogether warm.

"Are you all right darling?" It was my best friend Plantagenet. "You sound upset. Did I wake you? I'm so sorry. I just heard the news. They found a body in your store?"

I plunked myself back down in my chair and took a sip of brandy while Buckingham resumed his spot on my lap.

"Yes, a man died here earlier tonight. I let the storytelling people from the coffee house on the corner use my courtyard because they had a leaky grease trap, whatever that means. I wanted to be a good neighbor, and Lupe was desperate. But after the show, one of the story-tellers dropped dead, and there was some blood, but not like with a stabbing. A medical emergency, the paramedics said. It's all very sad, but for me, it's more of a nuisance than anything."

"Are you sure? Your voice sounds shaky."

I told him about Irene's visit. "I don't know why she had to bring Ronzo into it. All that silliness about abusers and poison and injec-tions. I have no idea what she could have against Ronzo. Maybe his New Jersey accent? Some people find that off-putting, I guess."

"Doesn't Ronzo read Tarot? Maybe it's professional rivalry."

That actually made sense. It was the first thing that had made sense all evening.

"Has Ronzo found his own apartment yet? You do sound stressed. Your tiny cottage simply isn't made for two people."

"Especially two people living on different timetables. He gets home from his gigs with the band at midnight and wants to cuddle. I want to hit him on the head with a lamp. Then I get up at seven and he wants to hit me with the lamp."

"Really? Has he ever…"

"No! no! Absolutely not. It's a metaphorical lamp."

"Maybe that was a metaphorical poison injection Irene was talking about. She did say it was a metaphorical elf, didn't she?"

"I guess. I don't know. I'm going to sleep now, Plant."

"Goodnight darling. No more elves or corpses tonight, promise?'

"I promise." I clicked off the phone and evicted Buckingham from my lap.

Then there it was. Another knock on the door.

six

· · ·

The No-Show Girl

opened the door to a red-faced Lupe. She still towered over me, even though she'd changed into flats.

Buckingham darted in the direction of the bedroom. Lupe's energy was too much for him.

I did not invite her in. I held my ground like some farm wife keeping the chickens out of her kitchen. I was that tired.

Her eyes were dry, but the evidence of recent tears was there. And plenty of anger. She hissed her words through clenched teeth.

"These bastards won't stop!" She held out her phone to show a series of texts. "They're texting me saying that I somehow offed Boyd! And the café landline is ringing off the damn hook. They're calling me trashy names and screaming crazy curses at me. I don't even know who they are."

I took her phone and scrolled through a few texts.

They were certainly terrifying and mostly incoherent, but I noticed several of them mentioned vaccines.

"Are you an anti-vaxxer, Lupe?" I hoped not. I did not need a case of the plague on top of everything else.

"No. They are. Scroll down. They are one-hundred percent batshit. Is that brandy? I could use a brandy."

She walked right past me into the kitchen and helped herself to a hefty snifter-full. After taking a gulp she plunked herself down at my dining table. My own glass was empty, so I refilled it and joined her. I had to feel sympathy. I'd been the object of some unpleasantness from social media over some fake photos of me from my Manners Doctor days, and people like this had destroyed Ronzo's life when he was a reviewer for *Rolling Stone*.

"I'm sorry, Lupe. It's so unfair to get this on top of losing Boyd. Do you have any idea what it's about?"

"I guess some news thing was on Twitter saying Boyd 'died suddenly.' Those are trigger words for the anti-vax trolls these days. If anybody dies suddenly, they blame it on vaccines no matter what the real cause of death turns out to be. By the time the autopsy results come in, they've been telling the lie for days and nobody knows what's real and what isn't."

I took a sip from my snifter. I didn't really need any more alcohol, but here we were. I wasn't going to see my bed for a while.

"But why do they accuse you? You own a café, not a health clinic."

"I have a sign left over from the pandemic days asking people who aren't vaxxed to sit on the patio. I don't enforce it. Just a request. But it makes some creeps mad even though the patio has heat lamps and it's real nice. Well, when the grease trap isn't leaking. Oh, my god, the grease trap!" She covered her face with her hands. "Damn. I'd almost forgotten. One more thing for me to worry about." She gulped brandy. "Do you suppose Boyd was murdered, for real?"

I patted her hand. "I have no idea. It's what Irene thinks. But the paramedics said it was a 'medical emergency.' That doesn't sound like murder to me. Boyd seemed hyper early in the evening. Do you know if he had high blood pressure? He might have had a stroke."

She gave me a funny look. "What did Irene say? Did she read something in her Tarot cards? I saw her leaving here with that southern guy in the captain's hat. What did she tell you?"

"Not the cards. An elf. An elf in the Elfin Forest told her Boyd was going to die and she thinks, um, well… she seems to be kind of delusional." I took a quick sip of brandy rather than speak Irene's accusation of Ronzo out loud. It was too absurd to think Ronzo could be a murderer. "So you don't know if Boyd had high blood pressure?"

Lupe sighed. "I don't know anything about him, really. Not the person he is now. All I know is that we had a fabulous week together in Atlantic City fifteen years ago. Then I heard rumors from some of the girls at the casino that he liked to beat up women. So when Boyd and me were supposed to get together for our last date — I stood him up. Totally ghosted the man. I've always felt bad about it. Then when I saw he was on the storytelling circuit here in California — I thought maybe it was my chance to apologize. So maybe he'd remember me as a nice showgirl, not a no-show girl. But you know what, hon?" She grabbed my hand.

I shook my head, not sure I wanted to hear the "what."

"It turned out he didn't even remember I stood him up! Seriously. I've been carrying around all that damn guilt for fifteen years. In fact, we're gonna go whale watching tomorrow…we were, I mean. Oh, Jeez." She covered her face again and gave a hiccup as if she were about to cry.

Her phone pinged. She shoved it toward me.

"I can't answer it. Can you look and see if it's another wacko? I hate this crap. I'll have to get a new phone to talk to my real friends."

I looked at her new text message and laughed. "Oh my! Apparently, you're an alien lizard person who has dalliances with the Duchess of Sussex."

She started to giggle and reached for the phone. "Oh, my Lord! I'm a lesbian space lizard? Getting it on with Meghan Markle? Call TMZ! I can make millions selling my story!" She was laughing harder now, and didn't seem able to stop. She was overcome with peal after peal of laughter.

Her giggles were infectious. I started laughing too.

The door banged open. It was Ronzo. He looked angry for a moment, but then gave us a big grin as he set down his guitar case.

"So you're celebrating? Ding dong, the bastard's dead? I thought you liked Boyd Ferrell, Lupe. Yeah, we heard the news over at Jack's. We got any beer?"

I jumped to my feet and gave him a hug, mostly to silence him.

"I think you've got one more bottle of 805 in the fridge. But we're not celebrating the fact Boyd's dead. Lupe is devastated." I gave him a pointed look. "She's also being harassed. Somebody on social media blames her for Boyd's death and she's getting threatening phone calls and texts."

"Yeah. They think I killed him with a vaccine 'cause I'm a lesbian lizard from outer space. And I'm banging Meghan Markle." Lupe lifted her glass and gave a dark laugh.

"Well, Montecito is only two hours away. I guess you two could sneak around when Prince Harry's out of town." Ronzo gave us another grin before going to the fridge for his beer.

Lupe drained her snifter. "Well, I gotta go, you two. I didn't realize how late it is. Must be past midnight. I gotta hope the wackos don't show up at my house. Thanks for cheering me up, hon." She gave my arm a pat.

After she left, Ronzo stood behind my chair and rubbed my shoulders. Then he bent down and kissed the top of my head. I grabbed his hand and kissed it. I really did love the man.

He sat in the chair next to me and gave me a dark look that chilled me down to my toes. What I saw in that look could almost make me believe Irene's accusations.

"Camilla, we have to talk."

seven

. . .

On the Road Again

 took a gulp of brandy as Ronzo and I sat in awkward silence. I could see he was having trouble finding words to convey the bad news. Whatever that news was. My brain kept zooming to Irene's bizarre ramblings about how Ronzo killed Boyd Ferrell. Ronzo and I had been long-distance lovers for years, and live-in partners for three months. But did I really know this man at all?

"Is this about Boyd?" I looked directly at Ronzo. "Do you have something to tell me about Boyd Ferrell? Irene thinks he was murdered."

"Irene's a flake." Ronzo laughed. "Her readings are B.S. I wouldn't be surprised if somebody whacked Boyd — he sure deserved it — but Irene isn't going to get any insight from the cards the way she reads them." He took a swig from the beer bottle. "No. This is about Cassius. You know, Cassius Burgh, the guy you sent over to Fisherman Jack's to find me?"

"The well-dressed one? Of course I remember. There aren't a lot of men wearing tailor-made suits and Bruno Maglis around here. He seemed to be friendly with Boyd."

Ronzo gave me a funny look. "Friendly? Not hardly. He hates the guy. With good reason. The three of us all worked in a casino in Atlantic City about fifteen years ago. I was right out of the army, working security, watching out for card counters and other cheaters. Cassius worked for the entertainment director, helping to book the acts, and keeping the artists happy. Boyd was security, too, but he was just muscle. A bouncer. One night he attacked one of the showgirls named Verline, claiming she stole some chips. He broke both her legs so she could never dance again. Cassius had a real jones for Verline. She was hot and real sweet. He says he never really got over her."

"That's tragic. It sounds as if Boyd was a thoroughly bad man. Poor Verline." This night's mood was getting darker by the minute. I hoped Ronzo would get to the point soon. I had to stifle a yawn.

"Yeah," he said. "She ghosted Cassius after she got out of the hospital, but he kept looking for her."

"I hope he finds her." I needed to lighten the conversation. "Isn't it strange you three ended up here in a little beach town on the other side of the continent? Kind of a weird coincidence."

"Not that weird." Ronzo sat back in his chair. "Cassius was already going to stop here on his way to San Francisco to see me, and he'd caught some of the Moth ads, so he knew Boyd would be here. Then he recognized Lupe's name. Lupe used to hang out with Verline back when. Not a lot of people named Lupe Sorensen, so he figured it had to be her."

I perked up. "So Lupe could tell Cassius where Verline is?"

"Yeah. That's what he hoped." Ronzo looked down at his beer. "But she had bad news. Verline is dead and buried somewhere in the Caribbean where her family came from. I guess she OD'd a couple of years after the beating. Lupe said she got into the drugs because she was always in pain."

I was getting whiplash from this story. "That's awful. And Cassius only found this out tonight?" I wasn't going to say it out loud, but that sounded like a powerful motive for murder. If there had been a murder, which I really didn't want to believe.

Ronzo gave a distracted nod. His mind must have been back in New Jersey in the old days.

"But you and Cassius kept in touch?"

"No, but he followed my blog back when I wrote for *Rolling Stone,* then he saw me on Jonathan Kahn's TV show talking about cancel culture last summer. When he heard I was playing in Morro Bay, he decided to stop by on his way from LA to San Francisco. He works for Pacific Records now."

"So you two are having kind of a reunion?" I took a sip of brandy and breathed a sigh of relief. This was hardly bad news. As long as he hadn't invited Cassius to stay here. This place was snug for two and would be claustrophobic for three.

Buckingham seemed to sense a lessening of tension and ventured out from the bedroom again. He jumped on Ronzo's lap.

"Yeah. We get along good." Ronzo gave Buckingham a pat. "Real good. He likes my taste in music." Ronzo still looked unsettled in his chair, as if he were about to jump up and run.

I tried to soothe him. "That's marvelous! It must be great to get some validation after all the hell you've gone through. Is Cassius going to stay long?"

"No. That's the thing. He's leaving right now. He has meetings in San Francisco in the morning."

"That's a shame." I still couldn't figure out what was making Ronzo so glum.

"Yeah, well, thing is, he's offered me a job. As an A&R Rep — like a talent scout for bands. These jobs pay pretty good and they're hard to get."

I sprang to my feet and gave him a hug. "That is fantastic! What a great job for you!"

"You're okay with it?" He looked up at me and took my hands. "I know I just moved here, and we had all those plans to start up the Tarot readings again, and you'll be on your own in the store..."

"Take the job, Ronzo." I leaned down and kissed his forehead. "But now let's get some sleep. It's been a long, long day."

He lifted Buckingham and set him on the floor. "That's the thing. I have to go now. Cassius is gonna pick me up in about fifteen minutes. I gotta throw some things in a suitcase." He took his phone out of his pocket to check the time.

Thunk. Suddenly I wasn't so happy for him. Or for me. My boyfriend was leaving me. Right now.

"When will you be back?"

"I don't have a clue. He wants me to fly to New York on Tuesday."

Buckingham let out a plaintive meow. Expressing exactly how I felt.

eight

· · ·

Magic in the Mess

I sleepwalked through the next morning, sleep-deprived and Ronzo-deprived, feeling like a zombie in desperate need of some brains.

Around noon, the store filled with reporters and photographers who wanted to see the place where Boyd Ferrell died. It seemed he was much more famous for his connections to Bon Jovi than for his NPR appearances, and the reporters were rock and roll types — pushy and out of place in a bookstore.

Much of the courtyard was still surrounded by police crime scene tape, and all the reporters could photograph was a few bloody bricks. Which I guess is why they all wanted to interview me to get my take on Boyd's death. As if I had one. But I had to tell my "story" over and over again:

"After the Moth event, Boyd Ferrell sat in my courtyard looking bored, while idiots surrounded him and endlessly told him their own stories. But it turned out he wasn't bored — he was dead. The end."

In the midst of it all, I was relieved to see the friendly face of Dan Fiedler, the Library Friend. I couldn't even speak to him because my check-out counter was blocked by reporters, but he managed to make his way to the desk, squeezing between the pushier gossip mongers.

He grabbed my hand and put something in it. I gave him a puzzled look, but all he did was grin.

He mouthed the words "I'll be back later."

As a man from a tabloid asked me if I'd been "romantically involved with Boyd Ferrell," I looked at the object in my hand. It was a single Dove dark chocolate square. My favorite. As the man nattered on, I unwrapped the chocolate. Inside was Dove's fortune-cookie message, "The magic is in the mess."

Usually I got encouraging Dove messages about taking a bubble bath or embracing my inner beauty, but this was even better. Magic. In the mess. Even this mess? I guess it could be true.

I took a bite of the chocolate and gave my tormenter a benign smile.

He turned away in anger. Poor man. What a way to make a living.

But I decided I should pay more attention to Dan Fiedler. He was actually quite a good-looking man. In his mid-fifties maybe, but fit and healthy with a full head of pure white hair. He often rode a bike to the store. Sold insurance or something. I remembered he'd said his wife had died recently. She must have been a big fan of Dove chocolates. What a lovely husband he must have been.

In the afternoon, after the commotion had died down, I had a rush of customers — not unusual for a Saturday afternoon — but enough that I realized I had to hire somebody to replace Ronzo immediately. If not sooner. I felt wrung out, like some old sponge. I also had no more paper bags under the counter and my pen was running out of ink.

I reminded myself nothing had really happened. A man had a weird stroke or something in my courtyard and then my boyfriend took a better paying job, but the whole thing felt apocalyptic.

When Dan Fiedler reappeared, this time with a giant chocolate chip cookie from Kat's Café across the street, I wanted to kiss him. I hadn't had time for lunch, and the half an English muffin I'd eaten for breakfast was a distant memory. What a nice man. He was the only person who'd seen me as a human being all day.

"Where's that boyfriend of yours?" Dan pushed the cookie bag in my direction. "I thought he helped out in the afternoons."

As I rang up a pile of self-help books for an older woman dressed in dramatic black, I managed to tell Dan about Ronzo's exciting new job. I tried to sound happy about it.

"Don't expect him to come back, sweetie," the woman in black said. "This little town will be way too tame for him now." She swooped out the door, whooshing the other customers aside, like a raven among nattering sparrows.

"Gloria could ruin anybody's day." Dan grinned. "She's bought the ladies' dress shop around the corner. Or rather, her rich husband bought it for her." He came around behind my desk. "How about I give you a hand? At least I can get you some more paper bags. It looks as if that was the last one."

"Back in my office." I gestured at the back of the store. "On the shelf behind the unpacked boxes. Could you find me a working pen, too?"

As Dan scurried off to my chaotic office, I wondered if the raven woman's observation was true. Was Ronzo gone for good? I guess that was the fear eating away at the pit of my stomach — that I'd been abandoned. Again. I didn't have a good record with my choices of male companionship.

I broke off a piece of cookie and popped it in my mouth. Not exactly a nutritious lunch, but it was all I was going to get. Dan came back with the bags and a pen from a dry cleaner in Midtown Manhattan. Which meant it had to be at least ten years old, left over from when I lived in New York. Dan then sweetly steered some tourists to the sports section and helped a teenager find the Young Adult romances.

I was about to thank him when my cell phone rang. It was Plantagenet.

"Hello, darling. I hope you haven't met with any metaphorical elves today. Are things all right over there?"

"Not really. It's a zoo. I don't suppose you could come over and help out for a few hours?"

"Darling, I've got rewrites for this Netflix script. They're waiting for it…"

"I can't find the book on 1960s cars!" a burly man leaned on the counter. "Will you get off the phone, girly?"

"I'll be right with you." I looked around for Dan, but he'd evaporated. "Plant, come if you can. Just for today. I'm totally overwhelmed." Oh, dear. I was being whiny now.

"I'm on my way." Plant was indeed a very good friend.

I managed to steer the burly man to the "automotive" section, where I hope he'd find the book on muscle cars he wanted.

Then a dithery woman came in and wanted the bestseller with the cover with the smoke on it. Rainbow smoke. She had no idea of the title and she didn't know the author. But it was a choice of Reese Witherspoon's book club and it was on TV. I asked if she knew the genre, or any of the words in the title, and she promptly burst into tears.

But a lovely woman I recognized as one of last night's storytellers took the woman by the hand and said, "I'll bet you want *Nine Perfect Strangers* by Liane Moriarty. I loved it." She took the weeping woman off to the women's fiction section.

But the burly man reappeared, angrier than ever.

"It's not there! I can't find anything about the 1964 Ford Fairlane. Or are you hiding the book from me on purpose?"

I tried to get him to calm down enough to give me an idea of the title he was looking for. He finally said it, and I looked it up, but found it was out of print.

"I'm so sorry. I'm afraid you'll have to look at secondary markets online."

"I'm not shopping in any damn secondary markets!" The man reached over the counter and grabbed my wrist. "You're going to get it for me, girly, or you're gonna regret it."

I kept pleading with him, trying to explain the difficulty of ordering out-of-print books. He wouldn't let go of my wrist. The pain was so bad, I had to sniff back tears.

"That's enough, sir. Camilla, do you want me to phone 911?"

Plant. To the rescue. My hero. The horrible man dropped my hand as Plant diplomatically tried to evict him from the store. But he lit into Plant with a hail of anti-gay slurs.

Suddenly Dan reappeared, and bravely took the man by the elbow and gave him an over-the-top pitch for the food at Lupe's café, He told him they had just made a batch of fresh homemade almond brittle and were giving free samples.

Lupe's almond brittle was indeed delicious, and its reputation did the trick. The man finally left, muttering obscenities as he went.

Plant was visibly shaken. "That's not what I expect in your bookstore, darling. What was that man's problem?"

"Spends too much time on Twitter," Dan said. "And those Internet hate sites. They keep stupid people loaded for bear all the time. They're told that everything wrong with their miserable lives is caused by some secret conspiracy. It's amazing they haven't killed us all."

"Do you suppose Boyd Ferrell was killed by somebody high on Internet hate and conspiracy theories?" I asked Dan after I rang up the weeping woman's Liane Moriarty paperback. Boyd dominated my thoughts, even with so much other stuff going on.

"I wouldn't be at all surprised." Dan gave a thin smile. "They're everywhere these days. Look at how poor Lupe is being harassed. You need to hire some help. That guy lost you some customers. I saw them leaving and complaining about the blue language."

Plant nodded in vigorous agreement. "You can't handle this amount of traffic by yourself. And I'm not going to be able to help while I'm working on this Netflix series. Is your arm all right?

I moved my bruised wrist as I cringed. Interviewing potential employees was always tedious and depressing.

"He didn't break anything, I guess. I guess I'll have to look on Craigslist for people wanting retail work."

"I have a better idea." Dan gave us a big smile. "I've been over at Lupe's talking to Felicity Grant. She works at the café four nights a week, plus a couple of mornings, but she needs more hours. Rent is so insane around here. What if she worked for you in the afternoons before she goes back to the café?"

"Felicity? Does she know anything about books?" Oh, dear. Did I really want to spend my afternoons with the sad muffin girl?

"She studied nursing at San Jose State. She must know something. And she's a good little worker. I'll tell her to come in on Monday."

A good little worker. I guess that's what I needed. Somebody to organize the mess. Maybe there wasn't any magic in it after all.

nine

. . .

Felicity Saves the Day

It wasn't until the following Monday that the coroner reported Boyd Ferrell's cause of death. It seemed Mr. Ferrell had been stabbed in the back of the neck with a thin, needle-like weapon, like a stiletto dagger, or an old-fashioned hatpin, which hit the *medulla oblongata*, causing his near-instant demise.

Murdered. Stabbed. In my courtyard. Boyd Ferrell had been murdered by somebody who had been here, on my property, less than two weeks ago. My hand started shaking as I grabbed my computer mouse, trying to find further information on the ancient bookstore iMac.

"Are you all right?" A customer put a book on the counter in front of me. "You're shaking. Do you need help?" The customer had a sweet face. I felt guilty for alarming her.

"I'm fine. Just read some scary news online. I guess all news is scary these days, isn't it?" I put on a big fake smile. I was not fine. Boyd's killer could be right here in my store, today. If he had died immediately from the stabbing, his killer would have been one of the dozen or so people who were left after the event was over. I tried to stifle a shudder as I glanced around the store.

"That's why I read historicals." The woman indicated her purchase

— a copy of Phillipa Gregory's latest. "All the bad guys in there are dead now."

I managed to laugh. Maybe I should get lost in a nice, juicy historical novel.

After I'd rung up her book, I emailed the news story to Ronzo, hoping he'd have time to talk about Boyd's murder — now the police knew it had been murder. Ronzo might like to know he'd been right all along. But he'd been so busy on his adventure in New York, he hadn't had time to send more than a quick text.

Which I have to admit I resented. He was going to be going to New York clubs every night, at Pacific Records' expense, and having a blast. Clubs I used to go to in another life. Like my old socialite / syndicated columnist self, he'd sleep through the morning, then go to fancy lunch meetings. Lovely for him. Miserable for me. I was feeling unanchored and abandoned.

I was also feeling some trepidation about hiring Felicity Grant to help in the store, even though I really needed the help. She'd obviously had a terrible life, poor thing, and had every right to be sad, but her negativity was not going to help me get over my own foul mood.

She arrived exactly on time at noon on Monday, wearing a tired gray sweater and faded Mom jeans. It might have been the same outfit she wore the night of the storytelling. No wonder she needed to work more hours. She couldn't even afford decent work clothes.

"Thank you so much for giving me this job!" Tears glistened in Felicity's eyes. "This is so perfect for me. I worked in a bookstore in the San Francisco Bay area when I was in college. And if I start here at twelve, I can get a parking spot before the rush at the café. I'm so grateful." She gestured out the window at the old gray Hyundai parked in front of the store. A sad car for a sad girl.

I gave her the usual tax forms to fill out and showed her around the store so she could direct customers to the right sections.

"Oh, I know the store pretty well," she said. "I could shelve some of those books, if you like."

A neglected cart piled with new arrivals stood by the remainder table in the back. I hated to have anybody shelve but me, but Felicity seemed so eager and knowledgeable, I thanked her and told her to go ahead.

Maybe this was going to work after all.

She emptied the cart in record time and came back to me at the check-out counter.

"Dan Fiedler told me you needed some help organizing things back here. Do you want me to start now?"

I was gift wrapping a Rachel Ray cookbook for a customer while another two stood waiting, but I hadn't trained Felicity on how to use the ancient cash register yet.

"Sure. Go ahead. I'd love to have things neater back here. Those shelves are so full of dust bunnies, they might fight back."

Felicity started to work on the file cabinet at the entrance to the desk area which was a combination of lost-and-found, wrapping supplies and junk drawer. Even I didn't know what was in there. Organizing it wasn't going to be easy. It was a bit annoying having her underfoot, but I was grateful to have somebody tackle the job. Organizing was not Ronzo's forte, and I never had time for clean-up myself.

The next customer came up to the desk with two of the latest James Pattersons. He leaned in to speak to me in a stage whisper.

"Did you hear the news? They're saying Boyd Ferrell was murdered. I was here — right out there in your courtyard last Friday night. I didn't see it. I guess I left before it happened. But the coroner says he was stabbed."

I nodded. "It's terribly upsetting, isn't it?"

I could sense Felicity stiffening as she worked on the file cabinet. She stood up with an abandoned Elmo doll in one hand and a broken pair of scissors in the other.

"Mr. Ferrell was murdered? Are you sure?" Her voice was high-pitched and wavery.

"Yeah. With a very thin stiletto blade. Sounds like a professional hit." The man wasn't whispering anymore. His voice boomed around the store. "Boyd Ferrell did five years in the pokey, you know. Probably made some enemies there."

"I heard he was killed with an old lady's hatpin." The woman behind him spoke up in a smug tone.

"A hatpin? That's BS." The Patterson reader turned to the woman with a scornful smirk. "Who do you know who uses hatpins these days?"

I gave them both a smile I hoped would calm the troubled waters.

"I'm not so worried about how it was done," I said. "But I'll feel a lot safer when they find out who it was that did it. And if the killer is still in the neighborhood." I reached out to pat Felicity's hand. I hoped she wouldn't burst into tears. Her lower lip was trembling.

"I'd like to know why," another woman said. "If we don't know the motive, we don't know if the murderer will strike again."

"Lupe will be so upset." Felicity's face had gone pale. She cuddled Elmo and handed me the scissors. "These things wouldn't cut hot butter."

I dropped the scissors in the trash can and told her she could take a break and help herself to coffee in the back room. "There's a cabinet back in the storeroom where you can put the lost-and-found items," I added, nodding at Elmo.

She gave me a grateful nod and scurried back to my cluttered office. I hoped she'd be able to find a clean coffee cup.

The hatpin woman gave me a copy of *People* magazine and two Romances to ring up. She watched the Patterson man as if she suspected him of carrying a stiletto himself.

"Well, I heard Boyd was killed because he witnessed a murder on a mysterious yacht moored illegally right out there in the bay." She spoke in a schoolmarmish tone as if we were all particularly slow children.

The Patterson man gave a snort. "I don't think so. Besides, it was Avalon harbor off Catalina. Besides, that was just a story he told at the Moth event — a kind of *Rear Window* thing — like the old Jimmy Stewart movie. He claimed it was true, but I doubt it."

The hatpin woman's face reddened. "Of course it's true. That's who killed him — the rich man with the yacht. And I saw him at the story-telling. He was wearing a captain's hat. My friend told me all about it. She doesn't lie!"

"I think we should wait until the police give us more information." I gave the hatpin woman a bag with her purchases. I didn't need a fistfight to break out in the middle of my store. And how ridiculous to imagine Bernard Lanier was the perpetrator because of his hat.

Luckily Felicity reappeared. She seemed to have cheered up and she almost smiled. She had a small brown bag with her.

"Would any of you like a sample of our almond brittle? We make it at the Otter Café on the corner." She held out the bag to the angry customers.

The two of them took several pieces and crunched away happily. We watched them exit the store and take off in opposite directions.

"That was brilliant!" I patted Felicity on the shoulder. "You're not only an organizer, but a peacemaker. I'm so glad you're here."

"I am too." Felicity gave me a genuine, actual smile and offered me some almond brittle.

It was crunchy and absolutely delicious.

"It's not me. It's the almond brittle," Felicity said. "It's like it has magical properties. When people crunch on it, they release their anger and forget what they were upset about."

"That must be why Dan sent my nasty customer to the café for almond brittle last week!"

"Oh, yes. Dan spends a lot of time in the café hanging out with Bernard. They both love the stuff."

"I'd better go get myself some tonight." I gave Felicity a sideways hug. "But I'll still need you to keep the peace around here. I think we'll make a great team."

ten

. . .

The Rich Man with the Yacht

hen Ronzo phoned me as I was closing up on Tuesday, I told him Boyd's death seemed to be a homicide and how everybody was speculating about the perpetrator. When I told him about the argument between the Patterson man and the hatpin woman, he gave a derisive laugh.

"She thinks Boyd was killed by a rich man with a yacht? I can think of a whole lot of people who might have killed Boyd Ferrell, but a yacht guy sounds pretty unlikely. Rich men liked Boyd. He was good at schmoozing them. And he only attacked women. Too much of a coward to attack a man."

I'd just turned the "closed" sign on the front door, and was getting ready to go home to my cottage, but it was wonderful to hear Ronzo's voice. I missed him terribly.

"Who do you think might have killed him? The coroner said death would have been instantaneous, so it had to be somebody who was here after the official part of the storytelling was over. Which is kind of scary."

"Was I there at that point?"

"I don't think so. You were probably long gone. People stayed in the courtyard and told Boyd their stories until after eleven." I thought back for a moment. "Although he sat there looking blank for a long time while they blabbered at him. Maybe he was already dead. I was half asleep, so I probably wouldn't have noticed if a vampire had flown in and bitten him on the neck."

"A vampire?" Ronzo gave a belly laugh. "Why not? If you ask me, it's more likely he was killed by a vampire than a rich man with a yacht. But then, it could have been Irene's elf. Maybe two elves in a trench coat?"

As if on cue, Irene appeared outside. She tried the locked door and then peered through the window. Obviously, she could see me, so I supposed I ought to at least speak to her. She looked distressed.

I had to interrupt Ronzo's laughing.

"I've got to go. Irene is here. I'll be sure to ask her if she saw any elves in trench coats at Friday's soirée."

Irene rushed in as soon as I opened the door. She did not look her best. Her usually braided gray hair hung loose and wispy around her shoulders, and she was wearing a man's hoodie sweatshirt and jeans, not her usual long dress and pretty scarves.

"Is he here? Has he been here?" Her eyes darted around the store. "Bernard? Has he been here? Did he tell you anything?"

"Bernard Lanier, your friend with the captain's hat? You can't find him? I thought you were living with him." Oh, my. The rich man with the yacht was missing? Maybe he did have something to do with Boyd's death.

Irene gave a huffy sigh. "I wasn't living with him like a lover, if that's what you're implying. We're just friends. I do Tarot readings for him. He likes me to use the antique decks. And he's crazy for crystals." She evicted Buckingham from the easy chair by the remainder table and collapsed into it. "I've been staying on the *Mary Sue* for a bit while I'm looking for a new apartment. My place over the surf shop was getting way too noisy. I think I've found a new place, but I left a bunch of stuff on the *Mary Sue*. And now he's gone. Totally gone! When did you last see him?"

This was a weird twist. Maybe he was the "rich man with a yacht" after all.

"I haven't seen Bernard since he came to get you after...after the

Moth event." I didn't want to bring up Boyd's death and further distress her. I gave her what I hoped was a reassuring smile "I'm sure he'll be back soon, though. He wouldn't abandon his yacht."

Buckingham snaked around my legs and meowed to remind me it was dinner time.

"Of course he wouldn't." Irene gave me an exasperated look. "He took it. The *Mary Sue*, the dinghy, everything. There's no sign he was ever here."

"And he didn't give you any idea he was planning to take the *Mary Sue* out of the harbor today? Maybe he just wanted to take her out for a fun trip."

"He doesn't sail for fun anymore. That Dan Fiedler keeps pestering him to take him out for a day on the open ocean. But Bernard says it makes him tired. He brought that boat all the way from New Orleans. The Panama Canal and everything. Took months and months. He says it aged him ten years."

"That's a long trip. I can imagine it was tiring." I was going to ask if he did it alone, but I was afraid I'd open a can of worms if there really had been a female companion who got dumped overboard in Avalon harbor.

"Exactly. That's why I can't understand why he took the boat out. But I did a reading and got the three of wands. It's the journey card. So I know he's traveling. But how could he? I left my most powerful Tarot decks in my cabin!" She looked as if she might burst into tears.

I was hungry and tired and needed to get off my feet, but it would have been terribly rude to abandon Irene while she was so distressed.

"Would you like to come back to my cottage for a glass of wine and maybe some crackers and cheese? I'm not sure what I have, but I'm sure I'll find something."

She accepted eagerly. After I fed Buckingham, I did manage to find some cheese and a few rice crackers and poured a couple of glasses of chardonnay. I had to move a pile of books to make room for her to sit on the couch.

"I wasn't expecting company," I explained.

"I guess I shouldn't have come...I didn't realize how late it was when I came by the store. I'm so freaked out about Bernard. He likes to hang out at your store, so I thought…"

"Actually, it's nice to have company right now." I suppose I was lying a little bit, since Irene was not the company I would have chosen, but I gave her a warm smile. "Earlier, I was thinking about how scary it was to be alone when Boyd's murderer is wandering around out there."

Irene set down her glass. "What now? You said murderer? I thought you were so sure it was a medical thing. Now you say Boyd was murdered? So did your boyfriend do it? Is that why he's gone? You kicked him out?"

I didn't dislike Irene, exactly, but she did have a habit saying awful things and expecting people to put up with them. I wondered if she did it to everybody, or if I was a particular target because of my Manners Doctor persona. I wondered, just for a second, what she'd think if the Manners Doctor told her to "F" off.

Instead, I took a calming sip of wine. Then another.

"The coroner has ruled Boyd's death a homicide," I said finally. "Mr. Ferrell was killed with a long, needle-like blade, and died almost instantly, which is why there wasn't a lot of blood."

"He was killed with a needle? Like a junkie would have?"

"More like a hat pin. That's what the coroner said. In fact, a woman who was in the store earlier said she'd heard Bernard had killed Boyd with a hat pin."

"Bernard?" Irene's voice went up an octave. "My Bernard?"

"Well, a rich man with a yacht. Who knows? Maybe Bernard took off in the *Mary Sue* because of that silly rumor, and he didn't have time to reach you. I'll bet he'll get in touch as soon as he can."

I drained my glass and stood, giving Irene a strong signal that it was time to go home, wherever that was. I did hope she wasn't going to ask to stay here.

Irene stood, but didn't move toward the door.

"Why on earth would Bernard kill Boyd Ferrell? He didn't even know who he was until I told him on the Moth night."

"I think the hatpin woman imagined that Boyd's *Rear Window* story about the man he saw killing a woman on a mysterious yacht was about Bernard."

"That was just a spooky story." Irene finally moved toward the door. "I doubt any of it was true."

But the expression on her face said something quite different.

eleven

. . .

Everything in its Place

Felicity was not the best salesperson I'd ever hired. Her unsmiling, perfunctory manner with customers came across as unfriendly. I knew I should talk to her about it, but she was so fragile, I feared she'd burst into tears.

She didn't reveal much about her current life. But she was full of wild stories about her homeless childhood, and the celebrities she knew in boarding school, but nothing about the present. I knew she lived "over the grade" in one of the inland towns that had slightly lower rents than the beaches. She seemed to live alone, which few people her age could afford. She claimed to have worked in bookstores sometime in her college days, but she showed remarkably little enthusiasm for literature.

I did know there were still some anti-vax harassers who were making Felicity's evening work at the Otter Café stressful and unpleasant. Even though Lupe had taken down the sign asking people to wear masks, and Boyd's "sudden death" had been ruled a homicide, the Twitter campaign blaming a vaccine was still going strong. One young man had started picketing the café with a sign that said, "Lupe Sorensen and Pfizer killed Boyd Ferrell."

And then there was Felicity's shelving problem. I'd let her shelve books twice before I realized she was haphazardly putting books in random sections where nobody would find them.

I sort of lost it when I found the new deluxe hardcover collection of Emily Dickinson's poetry in the Romance section, between two paperbacks whose covers sported shirtless men. It was late in the day, and my feet hurt, and I couldn't keep it in anymore. I walked over to the counter and gave her a forced smile.

"I'm finding some books in the wrong sections." I held up the Emily Dickinson book. "This should be shelved in Literature and Poetry."

She was cleaning the counter with Lysol for the fifth time that day. One thing Felicity was good at was keeping things sanitary — maybe because of her history of homelessness. She looked up and gave me a dark look that frightened me, until it suddenly morphed into an eye-roll.

"These people take a book from the shelf, flip through it with their greasy paws, then drop it wherever. How can you stand it? I found the brand-new Nora Roberts hardcover on the remainder table yesterday. It's so hard to keep everything in its place with that going on."

I laughed to cover my embarrassment. Of course it wasn't Felicity's fault. I was too quick to blame her. The truth was, Felicity was a fine employee by most standards. My discomfort probably came from missing Ronzo. Felicity showed up on time, kept things tidy and had organized the filing cabinet beautifully, throwing out all the outdated junk and making room for new paperwork. And she'd created a nice lost-and-found department in the utility room.

Also, she entertained me with amazing stories. Her childhood had been a roller-coaster. It seemed after her father abandoned her and her mother died of an overdose, her grandmother found her living on the streets of San Francisco and whisked her off to the elegant suburb of Atherton, where she lived happily until she was sent off to boarding school.

Her boarding school stories were much more exciting than anything I encountered in my prep school in Virginia. She'd hobnobbed with Thai princesses and movie stars' children and got to visit Thailand and was wined and dined by the royal family. The list of movie stars she'd met sounded like a list of Oscar nominees.

After that, she'd studied nursing at San Jose State, but she'd dropped out for some reason she wasn't prepared to talk about. "Too much blood," was all she would say.

Still, she wasn't the pathetic orphan she'd seemed to be at first, but I suppose her early years on the streets had created that victim persona she projected.

But she especially endeared herself to me because she never once initiated a conversation about Boyd Ferrell. Every person who came into the store thought Boyd's death was the only thing I'd want to talk about. They didn't understand that just because a murder happened on my property didn't make me an expert.

Not that there was much to talk about. The police had not named a suspect or "person of interest" or found a murder weapon. I'd personally looked all over the patio for anything like a stiletto or a hatpin, but all I found was an old crochet hook and a metal bookmark that said, "I'd rather be reading."

But every day of police silence brought wilder speculation from the general populace. A lot of people seemed to agree with our hatpin lady that Bernard Lanier had killed Boyd to keep him from talking about the murder he'd witnessed on Bernard's yacht. This theory gained momentum as Bernard and his yacht failed to reappear in Morro Bay harbor.

Then there were the more practical types who thought Boyd had been killed by a professional hit man, probably because of a prison dispute. They said the murderer would have to be well trained in anatomy to hit the *medulla oblongata* with one stab to the back of the neck. This contingent favored a stiletto as the murder weapon rather than an antique hatpin.

And then there was Irene, who luckily seemed to be alone in suspecting my Ronzo of killing him with some sort of drug delivery needle. It's true Ronzo had scuffled with Boyd right before his death, but so had Cassius Burgh. And it was Cassius who had the stronger motive, but somehow the primary suspect among the rumor-mongers was Ronzo. I guess his Tony Soprano accent made people suspect him of all sorts of nefarious deeds.

Personally, I was looking at Skip, the surfer with the Billabong hoodie — or maybe one of his friends. They were the ones who had clustered around Boyd, telling him their stories at great length. Skip and Felicity and the other café employees had been standing right behind Boyd before I left to go into my cottage. In the old days, I would have asked Ronzo to do some of his professional sleuthing to find out the backgrounds of those young men, but he was too busy to talk with me more than a few minutes a day, if he even picked up the phone.

Of course, I had no idea how Skip — or poor Felicity — or the others might have actually killed Boyd. I couldn't imagine any of those surfer dudes carrying an illegal stiletto or an antique hatpin in their boardshorts. And then there was the fact none of them had a motive…

"Can I get off at five instead of six on Saturday night?" Felicity gave me a self-deprecating smile as she put away the Lysol. "I've got a date to see a show in San Luis that night, and he wants to take me to dinner first. Lupe gave me the night off."

A date. What nice news. Maybe a new man in Felicity's life would give her a cheerier attitude. I did hope she'd change out of those Mom jeans, but of course it could be that her friend was into the lumpy look.

"Of course. I can spare you. Who's the lucky man?"

"Dan Fiedler." She shrugged. "He's always hitting on me, so finally I decided I should give him a chance. He's been out of town, but he said he should be back by Friday night."

Dan the Library Friend, the recent widower with the Dove chocolates. He had to be a good twenty years older than Felicity, but of course there was nothing wrong with that.

I should be happier about it, though. I feared I was developing something of a crush on him and his chocolates myself.

Was I feeling a little twinge of jealousy? That would be ridiculous. I had a boyfriend.

If the boyfriend would just come home soon.

twelve

. . .

The Return of the Mary Sue

*R*onzo had been getting happy. I could hear it in his voice when he phoned on Thursday evening. Now he was in Newark visiting his family after doing his music business things in New York over the weekend, and his cousins were feeding him familiar treats and taking him to old haunts. The grumpy-pants roommate I'd been dealing with for the last two months was gone.

"My cousin's wife made *povitica* and cherry strudel last night. I'm gonna gain twenty pounds." His voice had energy I hadn't heard from him in months. "And the night before, my aunt made *kremsnita*. I thought I'd died and gone to heaven. Did you know Croatian pastries are some of the best in the world? There's no place in California where you can get anything like this stuff. New Jersey has its perks. Is Morbid Bay still all fogged in?"

Yes, it was still foggy, chilly, and gray in Morro Bay — or "Morbid Bay" as Ronzo's musician friends called it. I had no idea what *povitica* and *kremsnita* were, but I could imagine they were delicious. He had a huge extended Croatian family in New Jersey.

I had to accept that Ronzo was happy because he was home. And home was not here. As I heard the joy in his voice, I wondered if I belonged here either. Whether I should have ever moved from New

York to California after my mother died — robbed of the family fortune.

And today, I'd twice managed to lose my coffee cup. It was on the desk in my office, and then it wasn't. It had migrated to the front desk. Then it reappeared in the office. I guessed maybe I had some kind of depression setting in that kept me from being present in my own life. I was too busy being sad.

In fact, everything here in Morbid Bay was sad. Felicity was chronically morose, and so was Lupe, apparently mourning the relationship with Boyd Ferrell that never was. And Irene was understandably distraught over Bernard's disappearance. Five days after he had sailed off into the Pacific mists aboard the *Mary Sue*, Bernard Lanier was still missing.

Even Plantagenet, usually my biggest cheerleader, wasn't a happy camper. The Netflix series he was writing for was taking all his time, with awful infighting going on with the writing team.

And the ever-present fog wasn't helping.

So I was pleasantly surprised on Saturday afternoon when Skip the surfer from the Otter Café came bouncing into the store asking for Irene, greeting me with a happy grin.

I'd been letting Irene do Tarot readings in my back utility room to help her with money so she could rent a new place, but she wasn't there at the moment. She'd been temporarily staying with her friend Alice since Bernard disappeared. Alice had a clifftop McMansion in Pismo Beach — apparently she'd rid herself of the abusive husband as well as the raccoons in the attic.

Thank goodness Irene had stopped saying Ronzo had anything to do with Boyd Ferrell's death. At least around me.

"The *Mary Sue*! It's back," Skip said. "I saw her chugging into the harbor early this morning. I wanted to make sure Irene knows. The boat's at anchor out in the bay, not in a slip, so I guess she'll have to wait until Bernard comes ashore in his dinghy, but Irene ought to be pretty happy."

I wasn't so sure. Bernard had shown truly bad manners when he took off without a word to Irene — leaving her with no home. She'd be foolish to take him back as a lover. If that's what he was. She was always cagey about their relationship.

Felicity came out of the utility room and gave Skip a skeptical look.

"Seriously? You think Irene wants that slime back in her life? He was a total bastard leaving her homeless without telling her. If you ask me, he's the one who killed Boyd Ferrell. He had the motive and he was right there when Boyd died. I'm sure the cops will arrest him when he comes ashore. Otherwise, why haven't they arrested anybody?"

I had to admit I'd had similar thoughts. The police were strangely silent about the murder. But if Boyd's story of seeing "a man on a yacht" kill a woman and throw her overboard were true, Bernard could have been that man. We now knew he had little respect for women — or anybody who cared about him.

Of course it had been Skip, not Bernard, who stood right behind Boyd during the after-party schmoozing. But I couldn't think of a motive for Lupe's employees to kill Boyd. Except maybe Skip's strange crush on Lupe. I knew May-December romances happened, but obviously Lupe did not reciprocate the young man's adoration.

"So you'll tell Irene the good news when she comes in, Camilla?" Skip bounced back out the door without acknowledging Felicity's rant. It was strange how concerned Skip was about Irene and Lupe when he was oblivious to women his own age. Not that his interest in Irene seemed at all romantic — more like a young man concerned for an aunt or a grandmother.

When Irene appeared about an hour later, in full New Age regalia — scarves wafting and bracelets jingling — she had the reaction to the news about the *Mary Sue* that I'd expected.

"Bernard had better have a damned good reason for the way he's behaved. I've been worried sick. If he imagines I'm going to go back on that boat, he has another think coming." She marched to the back room, her Tarot client in tow.

After her first reading, and again after the second, she came up to the desk and asked if Bernard had been in the store looking for her. Her eagerness to see him was painful to watch. Felicity gave me an eyeroll over the counter as she rang up a sale.

"He won't know where to find me since I'm staying with Alice, so he'll look either here or at the Otter Café," Irene said. "Make sure you phone me to let me know. He still has my best Tarot decks on that floating bucket of his."

"Methinks the lady doth protest too much," Felicity said, once Irene was out of earshot.

Methinks. Felicity said "methinks." She was always changing personas. Sometimes she sounded like a working-class girl from the Central Valley, and other times, she'd put on an erudite book-lover persona or start talking about meeting the Thai royal family.

She must have sensed my confusion.

"Dan Fiedler says that 'methinks' thing all the time. It's Shakespeare. But it looks like Irene's going to take that murdering bastard back, doesn't it? What an idiot. She reminds me of my mom, believing everything a man tells her."

That struck me as odd, too. Felicity had told everybody her mother died when she was ten.

That evening, when I called Plantagenet to talk about my grim day, he said Felicity's remark about her mother made perfect sense.

"Kids learn to be pretty perceptive when they have to take care of a parent at a young age. Roles get reversed."

"I guess so," I said. "But her stories are strange. They don't add up."

"I'd be a lot more worried about Irene than Felicity." Plant laughed. "Irene seems kind of unhinged to me. I could believe she killed Boyd Ferrell because she thought he was an elf or something. Are you sure you want her doing her New Age thing in your back room?"

"No, of course I don't want her back in that depressing room — with the mops and buckets and God knows what else. Ronzo was going to clean the place out, but he didn't get around to it before he left. But Irene was desperate. I'd have been rude to refuse."

"Camilla, there's such a thing as being too polite," Plant said. "Even the Manners Doctor needs boundaries."

"I know. Dan Fiedler said that too."

"Dan Fiedler seems like a good man. You should spend more time with him. I think he has a crush on you."

"Dan? But he's dating Felicity. And I have a boyfriend, you know."

Plant ignored my remark about Ronzo, which he did a lot these days. I guess he thought we were over. But he was being ridiculous about Dan Fiedler.

"Dan is dating Debbie Downer? On purpose?" Plant laughed again.

I had to laugh too. They seemed like an odd couple. But everybody was right. I needed boundaries. At the moment I felt as if I needed a big brick wall around my entire life. Since Boyd Ferrell's death, everybody I knew had gone bananas. Even Plantagenet. How ridiculous to think Dan had a crush on me.

thirteen

. . .

Poop Emoji

On Sunday afternoon, I was trying to take a "me" day to catch up on my reading and spend some time with Buckingham, who was missing Ronzo, too. The night before, I'd found Bucky in the closet sleeping on one of Ronzo's old socks that had escaped the laundry basket. The poor little guy would always love Ronzo best. Ronzo had raised him from a kitten.

We finally had a sunny day, and I normally would have enjoyed sitting out in my courtyard, but since Boyd Ferrell's death, the courtyard didn't feel like a safe space anymore.

When we heard frantic knocking on the front door, Buckingham looked up from my lap with heavily lidded eyes that seemed to say, "don't even think about answering that."

But I did. No matter what Plant and Dan said about boundaries, I couldn't be rude enough to ignore a needy person at my door.

It was Irene. She was back in jeans again today, wearing a faded blue windbreaker over a Morro Bay sweatshirt with a surfing otter on it.

She was not happy. Her face looked damp from recent tears.

"I'm waiting for Skip to come and get me," she said in a breathless voice. "Can I wait here? I was at the café, but Lupe kicked me out. She said she needed my table. She's got a big brunch crowd today." Irene shuffled into my living room and made herself at home on the couch. Buckingham scampered up to me to protest, but there wasn't much I could do.

"You and Skip are going somewhere together?" I said after a moment. A sixty-something Tarot reader and a twenty-something surfer made the oddest pair, but they were always together these days.

"He's borrowed a dinghy from a fisherman friend. We're going out to the *Mary Sue* to see what's what. I can't let Bernard ignore me like this. At least I can get my Tarot decks back. And my crystals. Some are quite valuable. And I have some clothes out there, too."

"So Bernard hasn't come ashore? And he still doesn't answer his phone?"

She shook her head. "No. He hasn't answered his phone since he disappeared. And nobody's seen him. Skip went down to the marina this morning and asked around. Everybody down there knows Bernard, but they haven't seen anyone aboard the *Mary Sue* since she came back yesterday morning."

"Maybe Bernard is sick?" I sat back in my reading chair, but Buckingham did not resume his spot on my lap. He lifted his tail and sauntered off to the bedroom, probably to sleep on Ronzo's still-unwashed sock. "If Bernard is sick, it would be tough to climb down to the dinghy and row ashore. He is an older man."

Irene brightened. "You're right. I should bring him some cchinacea and nettle tea just in case."

I was relieved to see Skip running through the courtyard, and opened the door before he banged on it.

"Irene, your ride is here," I said over my shoulder. I turned and gave Skip a smile.

I actually did hope Bernard was down with the flu. Then Irene could nurse him back to health and forgive him for whatever made him take off without a word. And Buckingham and I could have some alone time. It's one of the paradoxes of running a bookstore that you need lots of alone time to read books, but you also need to be with people all day in order to sell those books.

I wished Skip and Irene well and settled back in my chair. I was deep into my book when my phone dinged with Ronzo's special text ring. I grabbed the phone and clicked on the message, hoping it would give me good news about when he'd be coming home.

It didn't. In fact, the words made absolutely no sense.

"Ditching phone. Cops can trace this one. Will send new number when I get burner. Sorry. (Poop emoji) hitting the fan. Delete this. You never heard from me. I didn't do it. Love you. (Heart emoji.)"

I have no idea how long I sat staring at my phone, probably with my mouth hanging open. Finally I got it together enough to delete the message. What in God's name was happening? Ronzo had needed to go off the grid a few years ago when a vindictive band faked a video that made him look like a kitten murderer. But the band leader was in prison now. Had one of Ronzo's tough-guy cousins got him mixed up in something? It had to be pretty bad. Ronzo loved his iPhone. What could be horrible enough to make him "ditch" it?

Buckingham emerged from the bedroom and meowed. Zombified, I went to the fridge and filled his bowl with some Fancy Feast. He looked at it, then at me, and finally dug in.

That's when I realized it was only four o'clock, not close to his dinner time. It wasn't wine time, either, but I got a stemmed glass from the cupboard and filled it with what was left of the *sauvignon blanc* in the fridge.

I probably stared at the same page of my book for close to an hour, unable to make sense of the words, while dozens of worst-case-scenarios ran through my head. Had Ronzo run into his old love, the homicidal Lady Ruffina? Or maybe he'd reconnected with some of his bouncer friends from the casino and they were off on a secret caper? Or done something stupid with those cousins? Was he connected with Bernard Lanier's disappearance somehow, maybe through the casino? After all, Bernard had lived back east at some point. But he would have been moving in much more posh circles if he'd really met my mother.

Mercifully, my landline rang. I jumped, praying it was Ronzo, with an explanation of his mysterious text.

But it was Plantagenet. "Are you watching the evening news?" His voice sounded strained.

"Plant, you know I don't have cable TV anymore. Is something important going on?"

"Find the local TV station app on your laptop. This is bizarre. They're saying Ronson Zolek is a person of interest in Boyd Ferrell's murder. Do you know anything about this? Has Ronzo told you anything?"

Before I had time to lie about Ronzo's text, there was a heavy knock on my door. I looked out of the window and saw a police car in the driveway behind my Honda.

It seemed the evening news had come to me.

fourteen

. . .

The Missing

I managed to hide my shaking hands as I invited the police to sit in the living room. I knew most of the members of the Morro Bay police department, but these two were new to me. The unsmiling young officers, a man and a woman, were polite enough, but they obviously suspected I was hiding Ronzo.

I told them he had been gone for over a week to do some work for Pacific Records in New York. As soon as I mentioned Pacific Records, they started in with questions about Cassius Burgh. Luckily, I could honestly say I didn't know anything about him or his whereabouts. I'd only met him on the night of — I didn't say "the murder" — I called it "the Moth storytelling event."

But of course I got a lot more questions about that night — and the "altercation" involving Boyd Ferrell and Ronzo.

I was kind of glad they seemed to be suspicious of Cassius Burgh as well as Ronzo. I told them I knew the three men had history — having worked together many years ago in New Jersey. I didn't mention the unfortunate Verline, or Boyd's history of violence. The police probably knew those things, but I didn't want to bring them up if I didn't have to. After all, I had nothing enlightening to say about casinos in Atlantic City or abused showgirls. In the social circles I grew up in, New Jersey was simply an annoying toll road between New York and Philadelphia.

The male officer asked if he could look at Ronzo's possessions. I told him they were in the closet in the bedroom, but there weren't many. He'd thrown most of his clothes into his backpack, and taken his guitar as well.

The woman gave me a penetrating look.

"Ronson Zolek gave our officer this as his home address on the night of Mr. Ferrell's death, but his driver's license is from New Jersey. Does Mr. Zolek actually live here? Where does he live?"

"I guess I'm not sure." I found it difficult to maintain my polite smile.

"You're saying you don't have a clue where he is?"

I shook my head. "I don't. I don't know where he is, or when he's coming back, or if he's coming back." A little hiccup broke my voice, and I had to stifle tears. I was voicing the thing I'd been feeling for the last week but couldn't say out loud. I seriously didn't know if Ronzo had walked out of my life forever that night.

"In other words, the guy dumped you." The woman's tone was brutal.

I nodded, grabbed a tissue from a box on the end table, and blew my nose with more vigor than I'd intended. This wasn't going well.

The man came out of my bedroom and gave the woman a shrug.

"Nothing to see here," he said. "If Zolek ever lived here, he doesn't live here now. No razor. Only one toothbrush. Only a few men's clothes in the hamper."

He gave me a business card.

"Give me a call if you hear from him. It's very important that we speak with him concerning Boyd Ferrell's death."

The woman gave me a pitying smile and the two left without another word. I was too insignificant to question further — the useless dumped girlfriend.

I was left with an empty wine glass and the echo of the officer's words.

"If Zolek ever lived here, he doesn't live here now."

Ronzo was gone. Lost somewhere in the New Jersey underworld, I supposed. His text had made it clear I was not to try to contact him. Probably because of all this. He didn't want his phone calls to be traced. So he couldn't even talk to me. The explanatory phone call I'd hoped for wasn't going to happen. My life suddenly had a permanent Ronzo-shaped hole in it.

I grabbed a big wad of tissues and let myself have a noisy, ugly cry. Buckingham emerged from his sock-worshipping for a moment, gave me a disapproving look and turned back to the bedroom.

I was sure the Morro Bay police could not have paid attention to the evidence when they named Ronzo a suspect in Boyd's murder. Yes, Ronzo disliked Boyd intensely, but he left the Moth event earlier in the evening. There was a gathering around Boyd for at least an hour after that. All those people telling him their own stories. At least that's what I remembered. The whole situation was so surreal that actual reality seemed to be slipping away. Who was Ronzo? Was he a completely different person from the one I imagined? And if he wasn't really Ronzo, then who was I? The girlfriend of a murderer? Some gangster's moll?

I was not at all ready for company when Irene and Skip banged on my door a few minutes later.

Irene looked as if she needed a wad of tissues too.

"Bernard — he's not there!" She gave a heavy sigh. "Nobody is. It's a ghost ship. And the ghosts wouldn't talk to me. I did a reading and got nothing. Lots of Cups reversed. Empty vessels. Nobody knows how the *Mary Sue* even got into the harbor. It's like the ship came back all by itself."

I looked up at Skip, hoping he'd have something to say that would make a bit more sense.

"The dude has, like, evaporated." He shook his head in disbelief. "There's nobody aboard the *Mary Sue*. And the dinghy's still attached. Somebody must have brought the boat into the harbor, but it's like they got beamed aboard a space ship or something. Bernard Lanier is totally missing."

fifteen

. . .

Another Man Done Gone

"You and Irene are putting out too much negative energy," Felicity announced on Wednesday afternoon. "You both need to lighten up. Forget that Tony Soprano-wannabe guy. Come to the café tonight. There's a great new singer. Orion Jones. He's gorgeous. He's got an album out called *Another Man Done Gone*. It's on a real record label and everything. Pacific Records."

"Pacific Records? Are you sure?" This seemed like an odd coincidence. Was this Orion Jones mixed up with Cassius Burgh. Or, indeed, with Ronzo?

"Why would I say it if I wasn't sure?" Felicity had developed a habit of taking a snarky tone with me. "I'm not the one who's gone all delulu like you and Lupe and Irene. By the way, you left your phone in the back room this morning. You should pay more attention to your stuff."

Felicity gave one of her unfunny giggles and produced my phone from her pocket. Odd. I'd have sworn it had been right there on my desk all day.

"At least Lupe got it together to bake muffins for the café yesterday." Felicity exhaled a put-upon sigh. "But I had to make extra almond brittle again. We were totally out. She thought people shouldn't be crunching candy when Orion was singing, but everybody asks for the almond brittle, so I had to make it. Lupe acts so embarrassing around Orion. Did I mention the guy is super-hot? You've gotta come by."

How ironic that Felicity was the one who was trying to cheer us up. I had to give her some credit. She'd made a real effort to be nice to me since the news came out about Ronzo being a person of interest in Boyd's murder. She pointed out that it would be bad for my business if anybody knew my boyfriend was an accused murderer. And of course she was right.

I'd sleepwalked through the last two days, barely eating or sleeping. Could Ronzo really have killed Boyd Ferrell? He did hate the man. But this was my Ronzo. He didn't kill people. Not off the battlefield anyway. He also didn't disappear from my life with orders not to contact him. At least he never had before. So I didn't know what to think.

Dan Fiedler had brought me some more Dove chocolates, and a bit of the famous almond brittle. He probably knew I was terrified for Ronzo, but he had the good manners not to say anything on the subject. He didn't mention the Boyd Ferrell murder at all. He only talked about Bernard's strange disappearance and asked about Irene's state of mind.

But everybody else wanted to talk about Ronzo. I had to smile politely and feign complete ignorance. Sometimes Felicity would take the customer aside and whisper something to them. I knew she was trying to protect me from prying questions, but her interference was more embarrassing than the questions would have been.

Of course I hadn't heard from Ronzo himself. There hadn't been any more information in the news, either, and I hadn't had any more visits from the Morro Bay P.D.

Nobody had anything to report about the mysterious disappearance of Bernard Lanier either. After Irene reported him as a missing person on Sunday, his picture had been in all the local news outlets, but nobody had seen a glimpse of him since the *Mary Sue* left the harbor over a week ago. And nobody knew who had piloted the boat back into the harbor on Saturday. Not an easy feat — it had to have been done by an experienced sailor. Dan said the harbormaster reported the moorage fees had been paid for the whole month, so they weren't investigating.

"You have to come tonight." Felicity kept her bouncy tone. "You should talk to Lupe. She's going totally bonkers. Now she's saying she knew Boyd was a creep all along and she's not sorry he's dead."

Oh, dear. I didn't need to spend time with another unhinged person. Not when I was feeling so unmoored myself.

"Speaking of bonkers —" Felicity lowered her voice. "A woman just came in and said she wanted to speak to the Manners Doctor. You know, the etiquette author? It was like she thought the author lived here. Maybe she thinks authors all live in bookstores inside their books?"

I looked into Felicity's big, blank face and realized she was serious. Did she really not know? I tried to smile.

"But I am the Manners Doctor. I wrote those books. *Good Manners for Bad Times, Manners Rx for Bridesmaids,* and *Rx for the Mother-of-the-Bride* — those are my biggest sellers. People want to be polite at funerals and weddings. That's why I have a special display of them on the bestsellers table. None of my books are actual bestsellers anymore, but people still buy them when they're planning a wedding or big event."

Felicity broke into more of her weird giggles.

"The Manners Doctor is a New York City socialite, Camilla. A rich old lady who wears designer clothes. Talk about bonkers! You know, I'm going to move those books right now. It would be so embarrassing if anybody else found out you're pretending to be her. I mean, my god, your shoes!"

I looked down at my feet. Yes, I had stopped wearing my designer shoes in the bookstore. When I'm on my feet for ten hours a day, I need comfort. So Ronzo had talked me into buying some comfy athletic sneakers. I thought they were rather cute, and they made my feet happy.

I stood in stunned silence as Felicity moved my books to the Self-Help section and put two James Pattersons where they had been. More of reality was slithering away. I had to talk to Plant. He was the only person who could help me get myself grounded. Unfortunately, he hadn't been able to talk much since he called with the horrible news about Ronzo. He'd seemed jumpy and eager to get back to his writing. I guess he was feeling a lot of pressure from his Netflix team.

The store was pretty empty — only two customers lingering in the Sci-Fi section. Felicity could take care of them.

I pulled my phone out of my pocket and rang Plantagenet. Unfortunately, the call went to voicemail. He must have turned off his phone so he could get his rewrites done. I left a voice message saying I needed some help coping with the news about Ronzo. And I refused to believe he was a murderer.

"I wouldn't go broadcasting that all over the store." Felicity had materialized on the other side of the counter. "I told you not to talk about it when we have customers."

She was right, of course. I asked if she'd be okay on her own for a few minutes. I needed to go to my cottage to try phoning Plant's land-line, even though I'd be interrupting his work. I really needed him right now. And I needed to tell him about Felicity's bizarre ideas about the Manners Doctor — out of her earshot.

Back in my cottage, I petted Buckingham while I dialed Plant's number. I'd give him five rings. If he didn't pick up, I'd know the pressure from the Netflix project really was too much.

I was about to hang up when a voice said, "Camilla, he's not here." It was Plant's husband Silas. He sounded even grumpier than usual.

"What do you mean by 'not here'? Did he go out? I thought he had a crazy amount of rewrites to do."

Silas spoke in a stiff, cold voice. "He's on his way to LA to stay with a friend. He says he can't get any work done here. You've got to stop bothering him. It's not his fault your boyfriend is a murderer."

Silas thought Ronzo was a murderer? He sounded like Felicity. Apparently everybody had tried and convicted my boyfriend.

I apologized, hung up and took a deep breath. It was stiff upper lip time. I fixed my make-up and walked my sneakered feet across the courtyard to the store. Maybe it was best that nobody knew the Manners Doctor had been living with an accused murderer. And maybe I wasn't the Manners Doctor anymore. My syndicated etiquette column was long dead, and I hadn't published a book in five years. My publishers at Sherwood, Ltd. were always about to go out of business, and maybe it would be better if they did.

Felicity greeted me with a strange hug. She wasn't usually a hugger.

"Have you...heard?" Her voice broke as she pulled away and sniffled.

"Is it Ronzo?" As soon as the words came out, I knew I shouldn't have said his name. Felicity wagged her finger and motioned at the customer over at the remainder table.

"No. It's Bernard. Lupe says they've found a body that looks like him in a cove down in Avila Beach. I don't know who's going to tell Irene." Felicity broke into not-entirely-convincing tears.

sixteen

. . .

Don't Worry; Be Happy

rion Jones was a tall young Black man with a square Harry Belafonte jaw, well-groomed dreads, and a movie-star smile. No wonder Lupe and Felicity were smitten by him. He had a lovely voice too.

It was Friday night and he was playing his Caribbean-flavored music and traditional blues on a vintage guitar out on the patio behind the café. He had drawn quite a crowd. I was happy Lupe seemed to have solved her grease trap problem, and her patio entertainment was back in full swing.

Not that I was in any kind of mood to hear "don't-worry-be-happy" Jamaican melodies or yearning love ballads. Mostly I wanted to find out if Irene was all right. Lupe and Felicity were busy with customers, but Irene was nowhere to be found. Neither was Skip. Maybe he'd taken her to identify Bernard's body.

I relaxed when Dan Fiedler sat at my table and put an arm around me.

"I heard about the body down in Avila. I know it's upsetting. They haven't identified it as Bernard for certain, have they?"

I told him I had no idea. And I had no idea of anything anymore. My world was a chaotic mess. This confession tumbled out, along with a few tears, and I felt like a complete idiot. I found myself crying into his friendly shoulder as Orion took a break. My sob escaped into the silence.

Of course that was when Felicity showed up.

"Well, aren't you two getting friendly," she said. "Is this something I should know about?"

Dan's reaction to her was bland, bordering on stand-offish. Maybe they weren't dating anymore?

"Could we have a couple of carrot muffins and a hot cider? What about you, Camilla? What would you like with your muffin?"

"Cider sounds good," I said. I wondered why Dan was treating Felicity like a generic waitress instead of his girlfriend. I'm afraid it pleased me.

"Sorry about that," Dan whispered as soon as Felicity was out of earshot. "She seems to think we're an item, and nothing could be further from the truth. She talked me into taking her to a play production a few nights ago — something of a disaster — but ever since, she's been acting like the wounded lover whenever I talk to another woman."

That was interesting. So Felicity had lied about Dan being smitten with her.

"I did notice." I gave him a noncommittal smile.

Dan laughed. "I think she's attempting to make me jealous by throwing herself at the talented young Orion over there." He indicated the counter where Orion was ordering a muffin from an over-friendly Felicity. "Not that he's likely to be interested. Our handsome minstrel looks way out of her league. And he's not much more than a kid."

I was trying to figure out a polite way to ask Dan to clarify his remark about the disastrous "play date." But just then Irene came wafting into the patio, hair and scarves streaming, with dramatic tears running down her cheeks. Skip followed, looking glum.

Dan ran to help her. He was so kind.

"It's him!" Irene announced. "The body. It's Bernard Lanier. My Bernard. I seem to be his next of kin around here. He has family somewhere, but I don't even know how to reach them to say he's dead. Bernard is dead. Somebody bashed him in the head and threw him overboard. He'd been in the water at least a week. He looked awful."

"Or the dude could have been swimming and hit his head on a rock. That's what the coroner guy said." Skip was obviously trying to be practical, but practicality was probably not something that appealed to Irene at this point.

"Swimming? Naked? All the way down in Avila?" Irene gave a tragic sniffle and threw herself into Dan's arms.

"Actually, it was Pirate's Cove. The nude beach," Skip said. "So it's not weird he'd ditched his clothes."

Irene grabbed my hand. "I'm so sorry I told the police your friend Ronson Zolek killed Boyd Ferrell. I really thought he did, with all the toxic things he said to the poor man. But now I know there's a serial killer on the loose, killing people willy-nilly, it looks like it can't be Mr. Zolek. He's still in New York, right?"

"Um, New Jersey, really —" I stopped myself. I didn't know if he was in New Jersey, or even still on the east coast, and if I did, I shouldn't let on. I should change the subject. "Irene, why do you say there's a serial killer? Do you think the same person killed Bernard as killed Boyd Ferrell?"

"Isn't that obvious?" Irene looked down at me as if I were a slow child. "Two murders in the same group of people who were at your Moth event — maybe more? How could that be a coincidence?"

Why did she think there were more deaths? I could think of lots of ways Bernard's death might have had nothing to do with Boyd Ferrell, including suicide, but mercifully Orion came back for his second set and conversation gave way to applause.

He was accompanied by a beaming Lupe, who took the mic and introduced Orion again, bringing on more applause. She did look at him with undisguised adoration. Didn't she realize he was young enough to be her son? Or maybe her grandson? Oh, well, some men have that effect on women. He didn't do it for me, although he was certainly beautiful.

Dan Fiedler, on the other hand, had a silver fox thing going on I found very attractive at the moment.

He returned a few minutes later, carrying a tray with two muffins and two steaming mugs of hot cider. Comfort food. That was it: Dan Fiedler made me feel comfortable. Like a dad. Or a brother. Neither of which I had.

"Felicity is sure Bernard didn't commit suicide." Dan handed me a mug of cider. "She told me he bought a whole pound of almond brittle the day before he disappeared." He gave a small laugh. "It's true that nobody's going to do himself in while he's eating almond brittle. It relieves tension, you see. All that crunching. So maybe Irene's right about the serial killer. I hope the local law enforcement guys are up to finding him. Or her."

I gave him a smile as I sipped cider.

Was there any truth to Irene's theory? Could there really be a serial killer? If Bernard's death was linked to Boyd Ferrell's, that would mean the killer was still here menacing the Central Coast. And Ronzo would be off the police radar and could come home. Or at least call me, for goodness' sake.

Not that I wanted to be happy about poor Bernard's death. He'd seemed like a good man. And a source of stability in Irene's life. Not that she'd been all that stable. Had she really convinced the police Ronzo was Boyd's murderer? If that had been the basis of their suspicions of Ronzo, they certainly had a flimsy case.

A case that would collapse if there was a serial killer at large. But it was damned scary if he was bumping off people from the Moth event. On the other hand, if Ronzo was no longer a suspect, things might get back to normal and maybe I could untangle all these confusing feelings I was having about Dan Fiedler. He did have the brightest blue eyes.

seventeen

. . .

The Lord of Cruelty

We left the café before Orion's last set. Dan had seen me yawning, and offered to walk me home. Only a few doors down the street, but it was a nice gesture.

"What do you think is going on with Lupe and Orion Jones?" I asked him as we crunched down my gravel driveway. "She seems to have a major crush on the man. Quite the May-December romance."

Dan laughed. "It's not a romance! Lupe is Orion's godmother. She and his mother were showgirls together back in Atlantic City. Lupe hasn't seen Orion since he was in diapers. She was thrilled to bits when he showed up here."

Her godchild. What I'd seen was maternal pride, not a schoolgirl crush. Now I felt like a nasty gossip.

"I'm so relieved. I was scared Boyd Ferrell's death had sent her off the deep end. I guess Felicity didn't know about their connection, when she told me it was a romance."

"Felicity knows." Dan's voice darkened. "Felicity knows a lot. Don't underestimate that woman."

He had more faith in Felicity's knowledge than I did. After all, she didn't even know I was the Manners Doctor. But of course I didn't say anything. That whole thing was too weird.

When we got to my door, I thought it would only be polite to offer Dan a glass of wine. I could use one myself.

He accepted with a warm grin. "I'd love one. Lupe has applied for a liquor license for the café, but those things take forever. I think they have to wait for some other café owner to die."

Dan sat on the couch and I poured some *pinot noir* into my inherited Lalique glasses. As I handed one to Dan, Buckingham jumped up on his lap and made himself at home.

"Buckingham is fond of men. Ronzo is his real owner. I hope you like cats."

Dan petted Buckingham, who immediately began to purr. "I have learned to appreciate cats. My late wife had quite a collection — mostly strays she'd rescued — but they all died from old age over the years, so I'm cat-less at the moment."

"Well, now you have a rent-a-cat." I settled into my reading chair across from the couch. Dan was attractive, but I still had a boyfriend, as far as I knew, so I didn't want to sit too close.

We'd had maybe two sips of wine before we heard footsteps in the gravel outside and frantic knocking on the door. Dan jumped up to greet Irene, who was looking even more teary and distraught than when she made her entrance into the café patio.

"I'm so sorry, Camilla. Skip told me not to tell you, but I must. The cards keep saying I should."

Dan put an arm around her.

"What is it? Is this more information about Bernard?"

Irene collapsed on the couch. "Not Bernard. The other one. There was another body at the morgue. They found two bodies down there at Pirate's Cove. The other one had been in the water even longer, so it was hard to identify. But they wanted me to look at both."

It sounded as if Irene's story would be a long one. It would only be polite to offer her some wine. I poured her a glass before I sat down again.

"That must have been hard for you, Irene," Dan said. "Bodies that have been in the water for a while can look pretty grotesque. And they're hard to identify."

"Well, I knew right away it wasn't Bernard." Irene accepted the wine with a small smile. "This man had long hair. Long, shaggy blond hair. And he was very fit." She gave me a pointed look. "Not that Bernard wasn't fit for his age. He was a very handsome man." Tears began to erupt and Dan somehow managed to produce a handkerchief.

Had Irene really come here at ten-thirty at night simply to further air her grief? I guess she needed an audience, but I was so tired of all the dramatics. I cringed as she pulled a deck of Tarot cards from one of her copious pockets.

"I'll do a reading for you again. It may tell me that I'm wrong, and then I'll shut up about all of it."

She carefully placed a scarf on the coffee table and dealt the cards in a cross-shaped "spread" I'd seen Ronzo use.

Buckingham gave the cards a cursory look and took off for the bedroom.

Dan perched on the other end of the couch, looking almost as uncomfortable as I felt.

When Irene finished, she gasped as if she were about to burst into tears and pointed to one of the cards. It showed a woman crying in bed with a bunch of swords hung on the wall above her.

"Goddess protect us. It's happened again! There it is. Your future."
"My future?"

"It's the nine of swords. They call that card the Lord of Cruelty. It means you're keeping a terrible secret. Living a nightmare. You need to watch out. I keep getting it every time I do a reading on you, Camilla. I'm so sorry."

I found it hard to say anything. I had no idea what she was apologizing for. There was no way she could have known the secret I was keeping for Ronzo.

Luckily Dan jumped in. "But what does it all mean, Irene? What does Camilla need to watch out for?"

"It's her friend Ronzo. I'm almost sure that other body at the morgue was Ronson Zolek. I didn't tell the coroner. I pretended I didn't recognize him. But under all that bloat, it was Ronzo's face. He'd been dead for over a week."

Over a week. It had been about two weeks ago that I got that last text from Ronzo — I thought from New Jersey. But he wouldn't say where he was. Could he have been right here? Did he have something to do with the mysterious comings and goings aboard Bernard's yacht? I looked at Irene's "cruelty" card and tried not to let out a scream.

eighteen

. . .

The Usual Suspects

I'm afraid I might have sounded a bit rude when I asked Dan and Irene to leave, but it was almost eleven, and I needed sleep. I also needed to yell into a pillow or something. Irene and her silly cards had to be wrong. The body Irene saw in the County morgue could not be Ronzo. She didn't mention his tattoo for one thing. He has a huge tattoo of a blue Stratocaster on his back. Kind of stands out.

I sat rooted to my chair, drinking the rest of the *pinot noir*, trying to remember how to breathe.

Buckingham knew I was stressed. He hovered around my feet, but didn't get up on my lap.

What I needed was to talk to Plantagenet, who always had something sensible to say. But I didn't even know where he was, and it was far too late anyway. I needed to deal with my anxieties all by myself.

"He's fine, isn't he?" I said to Buckingham. "Ronzo is alive and well back in New Jersey, hanging out with his cousins, playing pool in some dive bar or something."

Buckingham gave a small meow. I motioned for him to come up to my lap. He did, and started to purr. Okay. Buckingham thought Ronzo was fine.

I petted him, took another sip of wine, and decided to ignore everything that had transpired in the last hour. Irene was always a bit wacky, and Bernard's death had probably pushed her closer to the edge. Plus, she'd never liked Ronzo. First, she'd cast him as a murderer, then as a corpse. Maybe it was her way of dealing with a rival Tarot reader.

What I needed to do was figure out who really killed Boyd Ferrell. I'd been going about my business like some kind of zombie, trying to believe the police would come to their senses. They were obviously doing some very faulty detective work, trying to pin the crime on Ronzo and/or Cassius Burgh. Which was entirely stupid. The two men had already left the scene when the murder happened.

I could see why they'd have jumped to that conclusion, though. Ronzo did have that small altercation with Boyd, and it was no secret both men knew him — and hated him — back in New Jersey.

But it was perfectly clear they hadn't done it. Well, at least it was clear to me. Boyd Ferrell had been alive and well when Ronzo went back to play his last set at Fisherman Jack's. Well, I was pretty sure he'd been alive. That's when I'd escaped into my cottage. I supposed Mr. Burgh might have popped in to do a little murdering after that, then disappeared again, but it was highly unlikely. Somebody would have noticed. As the only Black person in the crowd, and the only man in a suit, he would have been highly noticeable.

But even if it were possible, Ronzo never would have agreed to go off to San Francisco with Mr. Burgh if he'd known the man was a murderer. Ronzo had some sense of self-preservation.

Although I had to admit the fact the two of them left town together — with such alarming haste — could look pretty suspicious to the police.

But I knew it had to be somebody else. Of course, even if I figured it out, the police wouldn't believe me. Unfortunately, I had a reputation as something of a flake with the Morro Bay P.D.

"Who?" I asked Buckingham. "And who killed Bernard Lanier? Was it the same person who killed Boyd Ferrell?"

Buckingham closed his eyes, as if to show he couldn't see how Boyd's murder could be linked to Bernard's watery demise.

And I didn't either.

Okay, that was settled. Now I should get out of my chair and into bed.

But I had a thought. What if Boyd's killer had been Bernard himself? That's what so many people had suspected in the beginning. There was that hatpin lady who was sure Bernard had been the killer — and the Patterson man, too. What if Boyd really had seen Bernard kill a woman on the deck of his yacht? What if that Moth story he told was actually about Bernard? He'd have had to be extremely reckless, to tell the story of witnessing a murder when the murderer was present, but "reckless" kind of defined Boyd.

So Bernard might have had a motive. And he certainly had opportunity. He had charmed his way around the group that night and spent considerable time chatting in Boyd's circle — standing close to him. Bernard was a man of the world with a murky past. He probably didn't kill with a ladies' hatpin as the rumor mill had it, but might have owned a stiletto.

One would assume the police had investigated him a bit, considering the rumors — and dismissed him as a suspect for some reason. But his death might change things.

Maybe someone wanted revenge.

Buckingham reappeared from the bedroom and meowed to remind me it was bedtime.

"Who?" I asked him. "Who had so much attachment to Boyd that they'd feel the need to kill his murderer?

Buckingham went back to his water bowl.

Thing was — not a lot of people had been fond of Boyd. In fact, I only knew one person who even liked him, and that was Lupe. But now she was saying she didn't. Could she have killed Bernard? It would have involved some fancy sailing, getting Bernard's yacht out of Morro Bay harbor, then down to Avila to dump Bernard's body, then back up to Morro Bay — with nobody seeing her on deck. Did she have any kind of sailing skills? Not likely if she had to pay for expensive whale-watching excursions.

I heard a knock on the door. Damn. Why hadn't I turned off the lights and gone to bed? Buckingham ran to the door in anticipation. He did that all the time now. The poor guy was obviously hoping Ronzo would magically reappear.

But it was Dan. He said he wanted to make sure I was all right after Irene's weird announcement.

I had a terrible urge to turn on the waterworks again and cry on his shoulder. Instead, I told him my thoughts about Bernard killing Boyd because of that story — and how it might be true. In which case, the culprit had to be somebody loyal to Boyd.

"Loyal to Boyd? Well, that wouldn't be Lupe." Dan made himself at home back in his spot on the couch. "Lupe's done a total about-face in her attitude toward Boyd. Now she's calling him a sleaze and a deadbeat."

Dan's wine glass stood unemptied where he'd left it, so I gave it a refresh from what was left in the bottle. It only seemed polite.

"Felicity said something about that too. What changed Lupe's mind?"

"Orion, I think." Dan took a sip from his glass. "Orion's mother was a good friend of Lupe's back at the New Jersey casino. Apparently Boyd beat her so badly it ruined her life and eventually killed her."

"Orion's mother? Was she named Verline?"

"What do you know about Verline?" Dan gave me a sharp look.

"Ronzo told me a little bit of the history — she was a showgirl Boyd beat so badly she could never dance again, and she eventually died of an overdose of painkillers."

"What happened to her was pretty grim." Dan looked away and shook his head. "I don't know how Lupe was prepared to forgive him."

"Is it possible Bernard knew Verline? That would have given him a motive that's less far-fetched than Boyd's 'Mists of Avalon' story."

Dan gave me a condescending smile. "Let's let Bernard rest for a while. At least you didn't believe Irene's bizarre idea that it was Ronzo's body at Pirate's Cove. That's why I wanted to check on you. I'm sure you know Ronzo is alive and well somewhere — right?"

"Oh yes!" I jumped in with that lie without even thinking.

"Are you sure you shouldn't tell the police where that is?" Dan's face was unsmiling and fierce as he looked me in the eye.

I retaliated with a Manners Doctor smile.

"Of course I'm sure. Ronzo doesn't kill people. Not off the battle-field. And Boyd wasn't worth his time. The police need to come up with a more reasonable suspect."

It was time for Dan to leave, even though his wine glass was still half full. I didn't like where his questions were going. I stood, and luckily Dan got the message.

"It's late." He was back to his smiling self. "I'd better be pedaling home."

"Thanks for checking on me." I smiled back.

But after he left, I wondered why he wanted to know Ronzo's whereabouts. And whether Dan himself might have had a motive to kill Boyd Ferrell. He'd seemed awfully upset when he talked about Verline.

Suddenly I didn't trust the man one bit.

nineteen

. . .

Muffins to Die For

The next day, I was almost happy to see Felicity when she came slumping into the store as I was changing the window display with spooky books for Halloween. It was slow for a Friday afternoon, so I asked her to do some dusting in the less-frequented sections, like Westerns and History.

I felt it was important to let her know I was in no danger of falling for her heartthrob, Dan. Since the store was nearly empty, I went ahead and told her the whole saga of Irene saying she saw Ronzo's body at the County morgue.

Felicity stopped her dusting to put her hands on her hips.

"Camilla, you have to stop listening to Irene. She's a fraud. An old lady doing card tricks. I don't know why you let her do those readings here. She's using you."

I dropped the copy of Stephen King's *If It Bleeds* that I was trying to place between a plastic witch and some fake fall leaves, and looked Felicity in the face.

"Do you really believe that? I had no idea you felt that way about Irene."

Felicity shook her head with vehemence. "It's really — like you don't know how to take care of yourself. That lady has red flags all over her."

I made another attempt at balancing the book on the fake leaves and took a breath. What she said hurt my feelings, but I realized she was right. Why had I let myself be so vulnerable since Ronzo left? Had I become so used to his protection that I forgot to protect myself?

"What about Dan?" I thought of his bizarre behavior last night. "Do you think he has red flags?"

"Duh." Felicity gave me one of her eye rolls as she took the book from me and placed it perfectly beside the plastic witch. "Dan is a predator. I liked him a lot at first, but he was grooming me. Now he's doing it to you. He pretends he cares so much about you and he gives you chocolate and makes you feel special. Then bam, he drops you."

The chocolate. She was right. When Dan gave me chocolate, I immediately thought he was interested in me. That's probably what happened to Felicity. She wasn't delusional at all. Dan was a manipulator and had made poor, lumpy Felicity feel wanted.

A customer who had been browsing the self-help section left without buying anything. I hoped our conversation hadn't driven her away. I used to be better about not gossiping in front of customers.

But now we were alone in the store. I could talk about what was really on my mind.

I went back to my desk and took a sip of the cold coffee I hadn't finished at lunch.

"Felicity, do you think Dan could have murdered Boyd Ferrell? Or Bernard Lanier?"

Felicity scrunched up her face for a few moments.

"Maybe." She nodded. "I really don't know who he is under all that goody-goody library guy talk. He says he's some kind of insurance guy, but I don't know. He doesn't seem to have an office. I know he doesn't like your friend Ronzo."

That had been obvious last night. "You do know that Ronzo didn't kill Boyd, don't you?"

Felicity put down her dust rag. "Of course. You said he left before it happened, right? He had another set to play at Fisherman Jack's."

"Thank you." I felt like hugging her. It was amazing that I'd been trusting Dan and not Felicity when things should have been the other way around.

"I don't think the police are doing their job investigating Boyd's death." I put a few fake leaves and a plastic black cat near the register. "I've been wracking my brain trying to figure out who really might have done it. The list of suspects is long, since everybody hated him."

"Everybody but Lupe. Except now she hates him too."

"Why is that?" I settled into my desk chair, even though Felicity had to stand. Bad manners, but necessary when there's only one chair. Well, there was the big reading chair, but a certain cat was napping in it.

"Orion." Felicity solved the problem by leaning on the desk. "I think Orion clued her in to how horribly Boyd had treated his mom, Verline. Verline and Lupe were besties back at the casino in New Jersey, and Boyd beat her so bad she got addicted to pain pills and died of an overdose, so Orion had to go into foster care, and it was horrible. Lupe never knew how horrible. Of course maybe..." Felicity stopped herself and picked up her dust rag again.

"Or maybe what?"

"I don't know. I have a feeling — this feeling that Lupe might have been faking how much she liked Boyd to begin with. Because she'd told me a little bit about what happened to Verline before the day Boyd arrived, and her whole body would tense up and she'd look so angry I was afraid she'd hit something."

This was startling news. "You think Lupe might have wanted to kill Boyd?" Dear Lord. That could be why she was so keen on inviting him in the first place. And why she was so devastated when she thought she'd have to cancel the storytelling. "Do you suppose she was going to fake a romantic interest in Boyd, then throw him off the whale watching boat or something?"

"Or something." Felicity gave a weird forced laugh. "Or I could be way off base. There were a lot of people at that event. It could have been anybody, I guess."

I wasn't going to let her stop at that point. "Did you see anybody else there who looked suspicious — who might have been at the event because they hated Boyd? Somebody who acted angry around him?"

"Well…" Felicity looked thoughtful. "There was Alice — you know that friend of Irene's who told the story about her husband letting raccoons loose in her attic so she'd think she had poltergeists? Alice had a fit about Boyd hogging all the carrot muffins. I thought she was going to hit him with her make-up bag or something."

I stifled a laugh. I didn't want to stop Felicity while she was as on a roll.

"Then there's Skip," she said. "What's up with him? He hangs out with old ladies all the time. Something's strange about him. He seemed friendly when I first went to work at the café, but then he got all weird and stand-offish."

"Skip certainly had access to Boyd that night. Do you think he could have secretly harbored a grudge against him? Maybe he had a secret crush on Lupe and didn't want Boyd and Lupe to become an item?"

Felicity gave me a funny look. "That's a stretch. But who knows? I wouldn't put it past him."

A couple of young women came in, giggling, and headed for the Colleen Hoover display at the front of the store. It was time to end our gossipy conversation.

"Well, I think we should keep our eyes on Raccoon Alice." I laughed. "Lupe's carrot muffins are definitely to die for."

But what I was thinking was that Lupe was looking more and more like a viable suspect. Felicity's revelations certainly changed everything.

twenty

. . .

Burn The Witch

fter hearing Felicity's story, I couldn't help thinking it was likely that Lupe was the one who had killed Boyd Ferrell. If she'd been such close friends with Verline that she'd been a godmother to Verline's child, she must have known that Boyd's beating had left Verline crippled and addicted to pain pills. Could Lupe really have been in love with such a man? Felicity didn't think so. And if Lupe secretly hated Boyd, why had she been so eager to bring him to her storytelling event?

It was possible she had lured him to his death.

It made sense that she'd want to kill him, if she thought he'd gotten away with Verline's murder. I did wish she hadn't decided to kill him in my courtyard, when I was doing her a nice favor, but I guess it wasn't her fault the old grease trap had sprung a leak.

Still, if Ronzo hadn't been accused of her crime, I'd almost have wanted Lupe to get away with it. Her tough girl persona frightened me sometimes, but she seemed a genuinely good person. She didn't deserve the curveballs life had thrown at her.

Like the looney-tunes anti-vaxxers who'd been harassing her since Boyd's death.

For the last few weeks, I'd been doing my best to ignore them. They were still picketing Lupe's café daily. There was a core of four or five regulars, mostly old hippies with scraggly beards and long, gray braids, who looked as if they had smoked away any working brain cells some time ago.

But on Saturday afternoon, the group swelled to a crowd, and a bunch of well-groomed younger people seemed to have taken over. Instead of half-heartedly waving a few cardboard signs that said "Do the Research," they had big poster-board placards that said things like, "Vaccines Killed Boyd Ferrell," "Jesus Wasn't Vaxxed," and, enigmatically, "Died Suddenly!"

By the time Felicity arrived for work, the crowd was shouting loud insults at all the passersby. Needless to say, we weren't getting much traffic in the bookstore.

"Call 911!" Felicity stumbled in the front door, looking terrified. "A woman assaulted me when I was walking from the café." She gave a dramatic gasp. "She said she got cramps just from looking at me so she knew I was vaxed. These loonies are getting scary."

I grabbed the keys from the register and locked the door. No point in staying open and giving the lunatics a chance to come in and harass us.

"A woman actually hit you? Do you have a bruise or anything we can show the police?" It was tough to tell if Felicity's slightly askew brown sweater had been tampered with or if that was simply part of her frump look.

"I don't know." Felicity pulled up the sleeve of her sweater, but there wasn't a mark on her. Her hand was shaking, so I knew she wasn't faking her terror, but I wasn't sure I could report an assault to the police.

I was scared, too. There was nothing but a glass door between us and the lunatics, and they seemed to be moving down the block toward us. They had been attacking Lupe based on the flimsiest of social media rumors. Apparently some Internet crazies had now decreed that anybody who "died suddenly" had been killed by a vaccine, whether they had been vaccinated or not. Social media was bringing an epidemic of superstition and ignorance to the whole world. It felt like we'd been plunged into the Dark Ages.

"Open up. Let me in!" A deep voice called from the courtyard in back.

We both froze as somebody pounded on the back door.

"Dear Lord. Are they going to break in the back? What do these people want?" I was as terrified as Felicity now. As much as I hated violence, I understood why some of the local merchants advocated keeping a gun.

"No. Wait. That's Orion's voice." Felicity seemed to have calmed down. "We'd better let him in. He's been helping Lupe keep the café open."

It was indeed Orion at the back door. He was half-carrying a bedraggled Lupe, who was dripping with water and smelled strangely of smoke and floor cleaner. The pretty silk kimono she wore over black leggings seemed to be soaked and singed black on the sleeves and hem. Her face was frozen in a look of sheer terror.

"Call the police," Orion ordered. "Is there some place Lupe can sit down? I gotta go. Me, I can't deal with cops, so I'm outta here."

I evicted Buckingham from the big reading chair and Orion set Lupe down.

"Do you want some water? Some tea?" I touched Lupe's hand, which was icy cold. She stared at me with dark, vacant eyes.

"She needs dry clothes," Orion said. "I had to throw a bucket of water on her. I was using it to wash the kitchen floor, so it's got soap in it. But they were trying to set her on fire."

We really were back in the Dark Ages. Complete with witch burning, apparently.

I heard Felicity talking to the 911 operator on the store's landline.

"They're already on their way." She hung up the phone. "I guess there have been a lot of complaints."

Lupe let out a sob. "I had no idea people could be that evil." She became a bit more animated and tears started to flow. "I went outside and tried to talk to them. I tried to explain I never even got my booster and I had no idea if Boyd was vaxed. But it was like trying to reason with a pack of rabid hyenas. Then some guy wearing a black mask pulls out a cigarette lighter and tries to set me on fire. He said his girlfriend was going to lose her baby because of me. Some writer named

Naomi Wolf told Twitter that standing next to a vaxxed person makes a woman have a miscarriage. These people are effing insane!"

I was happy to hear a police siren outside.

Felicity showed up with a glass of water for Lupe and I went to the desk for the tissue box.

"I don't know if I have any clothes that would fit you." I handed Lupe the tissue box. You're so tall." It would not have been polite to say I'm a size eight and she's got to wear at least a sixteen to fit over those linebacker shoulders.

She nodded as she let out a sob. I watched this big, tough woman crying like a terrified child, and felt a little guilty that I'd been imagining her to be a murderer.

There was a heavy knocking on our front door and I was glad to see a uniformed policeman motioning for me to unlock it. I was less glad to see several TV station trucks out in the street behind him.

I let the officer in and closed the door behind him quickly. Of course, that didn't keep some photographer from filming us through the window.

"I need to know if anybody here has been injured by the protesters," the officer said. I was glad to see it was Officer Pilchard.

"The area is being cleared," Officer Pilchard said. "Your business should be able to return to normal pretty soon."

He caught sight of Lupe, who gave a dramatic moan from the easy chair.

"Do you need an ambulance, Miss Sorensen?" he asked.

Lupe burst into a surprising smile.

"Officer almond brittle!" she said. "You'll be happy to know Felicity cooked up a fresh batch last night. I'll get you some if the crazies haven't looted the café."

"Your business is safe," the officer said. "They weren't able to get in, although we caught a few trying to break windows."

I realized I'd been pretty much holding my breath for the past half hour. I finally exhaled and collapsed in my desk chair.

We heard urgent pounding on the back door again. Officer Pilchard motioned us all to stay as he went to open it.

"Darling, it's me!" Plantagenet's voice called from the back hallway. "Tell the nice policeman I'm friend, not foe."

Plant ran in, Officer Pilchard lumbering behind him.

"Are you all right, darling? I was driving back from LA and heard about the protest on the radio. Lupe, are you injured?"

Lupe shook her head. "Just damp." She lifted her still dripping sleeve. "But I'll be back in fighting shape once I get dry." The tough-girl Lupe seemed to be back.

"If you folks are good, I've got some other people to check on," Officer Pilchard said. "Miss Sorensen, do you want me to escort you back to your café?"

"Yes, thanks." Lupe managed to stand. "I've got some fresh clothes in my office. I won't have to go around smelling of *eau de* Mr. Clean."

"Can I go too?" Felicity glanced at me. "You're not going to need me here, are you? I think I need to go home and lie down."

Plant took my hand as we watched the three of them leave the store and head to the café.

"So you're back from LA?" I squeezed his hand. "Thanks for coming over. It's been kind of a hair-raising day."

"I can imagine," he said. "But that's not the only reason I'm here. I've been doing some sleuthing. I have news about who might have killed Boyd Ferrell."

twenty-one

. . .

The Southern Gentleman

Plant pointed at the TV cameras outside.

"Since you're closed anyway, why don't we go back to your cottage, darling. I don't want Silas to catch a glimpse of me on a news video. I came straight here when I heard about your protest on the car radio, so he doesn't know I'm back."

Oh, dear. I so much hated getting caught up in their couple squabbles.

"Buckingham will appreciate that." I picked up my neglected cat. "Maybe you should phone Silas, just in case? I know he'll be worried."

"Not yet." Plant opened the back door for me. "I left in the middle of a fight, and he will want to continue it. Frankly, I'm not ready for drama right now. I need to decompress after the drive from LA. Besides, I have to tell you what I heard from the West Hollywood scuttlebutt." He gave an enigmatic smile.

Back at the cottage, I got a treat for Buckingham and put the kettle on for tea.

"Do you want regular tea, or Earl Grey?" I went to the cupboard for my good tea.

"Plant made a face. "Tea is fine, but how about something stronger? It's three-thirty. Nearly five o'clock." He gave a half-hearted laugh. "I can imagine you could use some wine, after all that drama with poor Lupe."

He was right. I was feeling pretty shaken. I got my bottle of *pinot grigio* out of the fridge and poured two glasses.

Plant accepted his with a smile and waited for me to sit. He was always so polite.

"Okay. Spill the tea, as the young people say." I settled into my reading chair. "What does West Hollywood say about Boyd Ferrell?"

"It's not exactly about Boyd. It's about the late Bernard Lanier. AKA Lucky Lanier, AKA Bernie Lane, AKA Boniface LeBlanc. The list goes on. Bernard's death made the LA papers and sparked all sorts of gossip. It seems Irene's deceased yachtsman was a notorious New Orleans gambler, con man, and jewel thief." Plant sat back and took a satisfied sip of wine.

Buckingham took the opportunity to jump on Plant's lap.

"Bernard was a career criminal?" This was an interesting tidbit. "I guess I shouldn't be surprised. He had that Southern Gentleman charm spread so thick every time you talked to him, that it was difficult to tell who was underneath it."

"Well, the who underneath was a scrappy Cajun who would do anything to get what he wanted."

"And he wanted a yacht?"

"Among other things. He won the yacht in a poker game, or so the story goes. He also wanted the wife of the yacht owner, whom he seems to have seduced away from the hapless loser. But the most impressive thing he seems to have wanted, was three of the biggest uncut diamonds in the world."

Oh, this was getting juicy.

"Diamonds? Bernard — or whatever his name was — had giant diamonds? He didn't seem that rich."

"That's because he couldn't sell them. He was waiting for the news of the theft to cool down."

"So Bernard outright stole these diamonds — he didn't win them in a poker game or anything?"

"Either he stole them, or the lady did. Or perhaps they were in a safe on the yacht when he took possession six months ago. I heard several conflicting stories. In any case, he and Madame Delacorte took off from New Orleans aboard the *Mary Sue* last April, and neither the lady nor the diamonds have been seen since they put into port on Catalina in July."

I took a gulp of wine. This story was getting kind of bonkers.

Plant lifted Buckingham and put him on the floor. "Sorry, Buck, but if Silas sees black cat hair on my trousers, he'll know where I've been." He brushed imagined cat hair from his khakis.

Buckingham gave us both a sulky look and sauntered off to my bedroom. Maybe he thought the story was too preposterous. It was melodramatic.

I put down my glass. "You're saying Bernard sailed here from New Orleans with his new girlfriend and her husband's diamonds, and somehow mislaid all of them on the way to Morro Bay?"

"The story is that he left New Orleans with them, and he was seen in Avalon on Catalina in July, but after that, the lady disappeared, and nobody knows where the diamonds went."

"She disappeared? Like she broke up with him, or she —" I hated to say what seemed inevitable now, but Plant voiced it.

"Or she might have been killed and thrown overboard somewhere near Avalon." Plant gave me an impish grin.

"And Boyd Ferrell, taking a nighttime kayak ride, might have seen the whole thing?" How could we be smiling? True or not, it was a tragic story.

"It does shine some light on Boyd's demise, doesn't it?" Plant gave a dry laugh. "At least for us. But of course it's simply rumors — hearsay. Gossip won't convince the police that Bernard killed Boyd. Unless we can find some actual evidence."

This was getting serious now. "How believable are the rumors? Do you personally think there's any truth to the story?" I wished I had some way to contact Ronzo and tell him about this. It might give him some hope.

"Enough people talked about Bernard winning the yacht in a poker game that I think that part is true. And it makes sense that he was a Cajun con man who reinvented himself as a southern gentleman gambler. But as far as the lady going overboard, we can only speculate."

We both looked at the front door as gravel crunched outside, followed by loud knocking.

"Camilla? Irene in there?" More knocking.

Plant got up and opened the door to Skip, who was wearing a new hoodie with a picture of Morro Rock on it.

"Irene?" Skip peered inside. "Has Irene been here?"

I shook my head.

Skip jumped from one foot to the other. "I can't find her. She's usually having coffee in the café in the afternoon, but it's empty. The place is open, but nobody's there. Those looney protesters scared everybody off. Now I don't know where Irene is. I hope she's not aboard the *Mary Sue*. Since they found Bernard's body, the police are calling the yacht a crime scene. She's been staying with Alice in Pismo, but Alice says she's not there. You guys haven't seen her either?"

I shook my head again.

Plant stood at the door. "Sorry, darling, I must fly. I really do need to get back to Silas. Thanks for the wine."

"Wine?" Skip said. "I could do with a glass. I've been kinda worried about that old lady. She said she talked to Bernard's ghost last night."

Plant rolled his eyes as he waved goodbye.

Skip sprawled on the couch and picked up the wine. I was a bit worried he might swig it straight out of the bottle, so I ran to the kitchen for another glass.

"Did Bernard's ghost tell her anything about who killed him?" I handed Skip the Lalique wine glass, realizing from his expression that he'd have been more comfortable with something less breakable.

"Yeah." Skip carefully poured wine up to the rim and took a big gulp. "He told her to ask the raccoons."

"Raccoons? Bernard's ghost told Irene that raccoons killed him?"

"I don't know about killing him. Irene only said Bernard told her to talk to the raccoons."

"Maybe she was talking about Raccoon Alice? People call her that sometimes."

"Alice? That lady is looney tunes. She thinks crystals can cure everything from cancer to crotch rot. She tried to get me to buy a crystal she said would protect me from HIV. Somebody finds out you're gay and immediately they want to talk about AIDS."

"Oh, yes, crystals." It was interesting to know Skip was gay, but I didn't particularly want to talk about sexually-transmitted diseases. "Irene and Bernard were hounding me to carry Alice's crystals in the store. Along with Tarot cards. They probably had a point. More people believe in that kind of superstitious nonsense than read books." I stopped myself. I might have been insulting Skip's beliefs. "Sorry."

"Don't stress." Skip laughed. "I'm not into that stuff. Not that it bothers me." He gulped down his wine and stood. "But it does bother me that whoever killed Bernard is still out there. Boyd Ferrell's killer, too. I don't think Irene is safe wandering around looking for talking raccoons."

I wasn't sure if I was safe, either. If Bernard had been murdered for some missing diamonds, where were they?

twenty-two

. . .

The Ten of Swords

*B*y the weekend, all the protester brouhaha seemed to have calmed down. And Irene had resurfaced after staying with a Tarot client. She and Alice made an appearance at the café on Sunday morning, telling wild tales about the two dead bodies found at Pirate's Cove. The one Irene thought was Ronzo turned out to be a notorious gay hustler from LA.

Felicity was full of all this news when she came in on Monday afternoon. It was amazing how gruesome news cheered her up. Her cheeks were pink and her eyes had lost that dead look.

"Irene's still a mess. I guess she really loved that phony, Bernard. People are saying he was gay, but obviously he went both ways."

"And the hustler from LA?" I kept my voice low, since there were customers in the back, endlessly perusing the remainder table. "Were he and Bernard, um, an item?"

This would explain why Plant's gay friends down in West Hollywood knew so much about Bernard's history. And Pirate's Cove had been a notorious hook-up spot for the gay community for decades.

"It's possible. That's what Lupe thinks. Maybe the hustler was the one who took the *Mary Sue* when Bernard disappeared."

"So maybe the hustler killed Bernard and took his yacht, and then somebody killed the hustler and dumped both bodies overboard at Pirate's Cove?"

Felicity laughed. "You got a good imagination there. You think some rando just got onboard the *Mary Sue* and killed two people for no reason?"

"Well, it could have been somebody looking for the diamonds."

As soon as I said this, I realized I shouldn't have. Felicity's expression changed. She looked at me as if I were certifiably bonkers.

"Diamonds? Now you're dreaming up diamonds? Bernard didn't hardly have anything, Irene says. He sure didn't have jewelry. He was barely paying his bills, and he might not even have had title to the *Mary Sue*, Irene was —"

Felicity stopped abruptly and put on a bland smile as Irene herself entered the store, with a mousy little woman in tow. Somebody I didn't know. Not the robust Alice.

"Can I use your back room to do a reading for my friend here? We ran into each other at the café, and she really needs a reading." Irene's tone was perky. She seemed to be overcoming her grief rather well.

I told her she and her client could use the room if they promised to ignore the mess. I hadn't touched the room in weeks.

"She seems to have cheered up," I said to Felicity *sotto voce* once Irene had closed the door.

"That's her phony Tarot reader voice." Felicity frowned. "I know she's crying inside."

"So who do you think killed Bernard?"

Felicity snorted. "Oh, don't ask me. I don't know anything." Her voice had gone back to her usual whine. "Nobody even told me about the diamonds, so I'm just a mushroom, sitting here in the dark. But it sure seems like it had to be the same person who killed Boyd. I mean, we had what — forty people at that Moth event? And two are murdered within weeks? It seems like they have to be related."

I pondered this as I hurried back to the desk to ring up some five-year-old bestsellers for two of the customers who had been browsing the remainder table. I'd rather forgotten them and hoped they hadn't heard our conversation. There was another customer back in the travel section, rustling around, but I couldn't see anybody. I hoped they hadn't heard either.

Once the two customers left, Felicity asked if she could get herself some coffee from the café. I had to let her. She was entitled to a break and the store's ancient Mr. Coffee and tired jar of Coffee-Mate could not compete with Lupe's lattes.

As Felicity disappeared down the street, I heard footsteps behind me. I turned and saw Dan Fiedler, wearing his Friends of the Library tee-shirt. He must have been the one who overheard our gossip. I felt my cheeks redden. I really had shown bad manners.

"Diamonds." he said. "What do you know about Bernard's diamonds, Camilla?" His voice was sharp as his eyes stared directly into mine. He might have been wearing the tee-shirt, but the affable mask he usually wore was off. He meant business. I wished I knew what that business was.

"Me? I don't know a thing." I decided to copy Felicity's fake-clueless tone. "My friend Plantagenet was down in West Hollywood and there are lots of rumors going around about Bernard Lanier, who was apparently some kind of con man from New Orleans. Plant said Bernard had stolen some diamonds, but now nobody knows where they are."

Dan gave me an unblinking stare for long enough to make me seriously uncomfortable, so I looked away. Did the man have a weapon? Was he about to do me in with a stiletto, like Boyd Ferrell?

"I haven't seen you around for the last few days Dan." I kept on my mask of cheery cluelessness. "Have you been out of town?"

"On and off." He was still giving me that look. "So it's Plantagenet who knows about the diamonds?"

OMG, had I just given a murderer a reason to kill Plant?

"No, no. Plant doesn't know a thing. Except how to pick up juicy gossip in West Hollywood. It seems Bernard was bisexual, and had been at some point a member of the Hollywood gay community."

"I don't believe you. Plant knows more, doesn't he?" Now Dan was coming at me, pushing his way behind the desk. I looked around for a weapon. All I could find was the pair of scissors we used for gift wrapping. I inched my hand toward the scissors as Dan came closer, in his menacing slow motion.

"Camilla, you'll be amazed at the reading I did for you!" Irene and her friend emerged from the back room. I'd almost forgotten they were there. "Dan? Is that you?" Irene made a bee-line for Dan and gave him a hug. "I haven't seen you around. You do know about Lupe, don't you? How she got attacked yesterday?"

Dan looked dazed for a moment. "Lupe? No. You'll have to tell me later. Now I've got to run…" He turned and nearly sprinted out of the store — looking as frightened by Irene as I'd been of him.

"Well, that was rude." Irene turned to her friend. "Don't you think he was rude?"

The mousy woman nodded.

"But I haven't told you about your reading, Camilla." Irene turned back to me and took her Tarot deck out of her purse. She removed the silk scarf she kept them wrapped in. "I did a simple three card reading for you, to thank you for letting me see my clients here again. But it's not good. I saw danger. Terrible danger for you. But not to worry. You'll escape in the nick of time. See?"

Irene picked three cards off the top of the deck.

"I've never dealt a spread like this," she said. "Not in all my years with the Tarot. It's all swords. Not any other minor or major arcana. It's the three, the ten, and the six. Now the first two, those are danger cards. The three means heartbreak — I guess that's when Ronzo left you. The ten means betrayal — you're about to be stabbed in the back. But the six means escape. See how the woman is sad, but the boat is taking her from rough seas to calm?"

I looked at the three cards and wished Ronzo was here. He could tell me if Irene was simply babbling, or if I should pay attention to this nonsense.

"So you're saying I just avoided being stabbed in the back?" I pointed at the ten of swords card, which pictured a man lying on the ground with ten swords stuck in his back.

"Yes. That's about the size of it. You could have been totally destroyed by somebody, but you escaped. The reading is probably about your friend Ronzo. I never have trusted that man."

I matched her fake smile with one of my own. But I knew that if I had been in danger, it wasn't from Ronzo, but from our mysterious Friend of the Library, Dan Fiedler.

twenty-three

. . .

Little Orphan Mary Sue

"How do we know Irene didn't kill Bernard?" Felicity burst out with this random question as we were closing up the store Monday evening.

I'd told her about Irene's bizarre Tarot reading, which Felicity pronounced "a load of poop." I tended to agree with her, but I didn't want to stoop to Irene-bashing.

I locked the front door and flipped the "open" sign to "closed," then turned back to Felicity.

"I can't believe Irene killed him. You could see she was fond of Bernard. And she was living aboard the *Mary Sue*. It would have made no sense for her to kill him and lose her home."

Felicity set down the pile of books she'd been collecting and reshelving.

"You said there were diamonds, didn't you? I could totally believe Irene would kill for a fortune in diamonds. She's so fake. She never lets anybody know what she's really thinking."

"She doesn't have any trouble telling me she thinks Ronzo is a dangerous lowlife." It was hard to think of Irene as inscrutable. She seemed like an open book to me. I was still much more suspicious of

Lupe, in spite of the fact I felt sympathy for the woman after the protester attack. Lupe certainly had motive to kill Boyd, and maybe Bernard had figured out she was the culprit, so she silenced him.

I took the cash drawer to the office to put in the safe. Felicity followed me.

"Yeah, well that's probably projection. Maybe she's the one who's a dangerous lowlife." Felicity laughed that hiccuppy laugh of hers. "I mean we don't know anything about her, except that she's hard up for money and talks a whole lot of crap. How old do you think she is? Like, fifty?"

Younger people have such trouble judging age. "No. I'd say she's well into her sixties. I think I read that Bernard was sixty-five."

Felicity gave me a skeptical look. She was skeptical of most things I said these days.

"I'll go shut down the computer and straighten the front desk," she said.

A moment later, there was a knock on the front door. I looked out the window and saw Plantagenet — with Silas, which was a good sign. They must have made up whatever quarrel it was that sent Plant down to LA.

I waved and reached for the keys.

As soon as I unlocked the door, the two men burst in, full of smiles and high energy.

"Finish up in here, darling. We're taking you to dinner. We had a craving for fish and chips, so we have to go to Dockside. There should be a great sunset over the bay tonight."

I gave both of them hugs and said I'd be ready right away. I needed to go back to my cottage to get a warm jacket and feed Buckingham.

Felicity appeared and I introduced her to Silas. I hoped she wouldn't say anything embarrassing or homophobic while I was gone.

But I needn't have worried. When I got back, wearing my new puffy winter jacket, she was chatting happily with them both.

"Felicity is going to join us." Plant gave an unironic smile. "Come on. There's usually a wait to get into Dockside."

I don't know why I felt such disappointment to hear Felicity was coming with us. I knew she was lonely, and it would have been ungracious to exclude her. I guess I'd had plenty of Felicity's company for the day, and mostly I wanted my friends all to myself. Which was selfish and rude of me. I guess I was feeling lonely with Ronzo gone. I worked up a smile and followed the three of them out the back door to the driveway where Silas's BMW was waiting.

When I saw Felicity all lit up with a happy grin, I felt like a terrible person. She was my employee after all, and I should be kind to her.

Dockside is an outdoor casual restaurant right on the water. Heat lamps kept us from freezing in the chilly October weather. We all ordered local beer and some of Dockside's halibut right off their boat. I ordered mine grilled with coleslaw. The rest of them got the traditional deep-fried.

As we waited, watching the magnificent sunset over the bay, Plant entertained us with more stories about Bernard and the girlfriend he may or may not have thrown into Avalon harbor. Then Plant asked Felicity if she had any theories about who killed Bernard.

I cringed and butted in, although I knew it was impolite. "Oh, she thinks Irene did it, but I disagree. Irene can be irritating, but I can't believe she's capable of murder."

Silas harumphed. "Anybody is capable of murder if they're triggered."

Plant leaned in toward Felicity. "Do you think Irene killed Boyd Ferrell, too?"

Felicity shook her head. "I thought the two deaths had to be linked, but I don't anymore. Now I think the person who killed Boyd Ferrell is Dan Fiedler."

Well. That was news to me. Was Dan being as creepy around her as he was with me?

"Dan Fiedler? The Friend of the Library?" Plant laughed. I hadn't told him about my recent run-ins with Dan. "What did he kill him with? Almond brittle? Dan was such a good guy, protecting us from the weirdos who invaded the bookstore on the day after the murder. I thought he was a good friend of yours, Camilla."

I hesitated as I chewed my coleslaw. "I've kind of changed my mind about him. He's way too interested in Bernard's diamonds. But if he killed anybody, I think it was Bernard, not Boyd."

"Why does everybody know about these diamonds but me?" Felicity's voice reverted to her grating whine.

"That's okay. I don't know about any diamonds, either." Silas patted her shoulder and gave her a warm smile.

Plant launched into the saga of the missing jewels. "Somebody said these diamonds are bigger than golf balls," he said as he concluded his tale. "But that's only a rumor. None of the people who told me the story had actually seen them."

"You mean nobody knows if these diamonds actually exist?" Felicity was obviously not impressed.

"But if they do, they must be somewhere on Bernard's yacht." Silas sat back, the sunset coloring his graying beard a rosy orange. "Who owns the yacht? Is it still in Morro Bay?"

Plant looked to me for information, but I couldn't help much.

"I don't think anybody knows right now. The boat is kind of an orphan. It's moored down by the marina, but the harbor patrol warned people not to go aboard until ownership is established."

"Did Bernard leave a will?" Silas gave me the same inquiring look, but all I could do was shrug.

"A will won't matter if the *Mary Sue* wasn't his to bequeath," Plant said. "Most people say he won it in a poker game, but there's another story that he stole it outright from his girlfriend's husband in New Orleans. And of course there's the problem of his name. Apparently he changed it so often, nobody knows his legal name, so even if he has the title, it might not be valid, if he signed it as Bernard Lanier."

"The police say the *Mary Sue* belongs to a professional gambler from New Orleans named Eugene Delacorte." This pronouncement came from none other than Dan Fiedler himself, suddenly silhouetted against the orange sky by our table. I saw Felicity flinch and felt a chill in spite of my warm jacket.

Plant and Silas greeted him warmly, but all Felicity and I could do was sit in uncomfortable silence.

I felt Dan's hand on my shoulder, heavy and cold. "Camilla, it sounds as if the local cops aren't all that interested in your boyfriend, Mr. Zolek, any more. You can stop pretending you don't know where he is."

I shivered in silence, but Felicity spoke up with her suddenly-welcome whine.

"She's not pretending, Dan, and it's mean of you to say so."

twenty-four

. . .

Negative Energy

Tuesday morning the store was nearly empty. But my brain was so muddled, all I could do was shelve books and pray for Ronzo to phone me. If he really was in the clear, he would call. If he wasn't, and I called him, the police might trace it, which could lead to catastrophe. Not that I knew if the phone number I had would reach him anymore.

Why did Dan Fiedler tell me Ronzo was no longer a suspect in Boyd's murder? What did he know? Was Dan hoping I'd contact Ronzo and get him out of hiding?

This was all so weird. The police couldn't suspect Ronzo had anything to do with Bernard's death or those mysterious diamonds. It would have been pretty tough for him to orchestrate all that from New Jersey. Or wherever he was. So maybe he wasn't a suspect in the other murder anymore. But I couldn't be sure.

A customer came in and marched right up to the checkout counter. Probably somebody with a book on order. I dropped my shelving and gave her a welcoming hello. The woman was tiny and her voice such a mousey squeak I couldn't make out what she was saying. She seemed to be asking for somebody named Crystal.

I slowly recognized her as Irene's client from last week.

"I want a reading with crystals," she repeated. "Irene used to put crystals there on the table with the cards. They clear the negative energy and promote healing. I think the energy in this place is very negative. You know, because of the murder."

"Crystals." I tried to figure out what to say next. I was embarrassingly ignorant of New Age lore. "Irene's friend Alice is a big fan of crystals. Bernard was too. They wanted me to carry them in the store, but I don't know enough about them. I'll let Irene know that you'd like a crystal-enhanced reading."

"Can't you do it? You must have some crystals here."

I'm afraid I let out a giggle. "Oh, no. You do not want me to try to read Tarot cards with or without crystals. Any more than you want to watch me compete in a gymnastics contest. Or fly an airplane. I do not have the foggiest idea how to do any of those things."

"But your boyfriend did. The one who sounded like Tony Soprano? I asked for a reading and told him I wanted crystals and he did the whole thing. With rose quartz, I think. Very cleansing. Excellent reading, too. Everything he predicted came true."

I leaned against the desk and took a breath. Did that actually happen? Alice had left some sample crystals here for Ronzo to look at when we were considering carrying New Age merchandise. Only a few weeks ago — although it felt like months.

"Isn't Ronzo wonderful?" I said with a dramatic sigh. "But he has a new job that takes him all over the country. I miss him so much." I let my eyes get misty.

"That's all right dear," she said. "Just tell Irene I want crystals next time."

Of course she left without buying a book. The New Age people usually did. Irene was right. I should carry cards and crystals and incense and astrology books — things that catered to this clientele. Silas would have a fit, of course. It had been his bookstore originally. He'd had a chain of them, but had sold off most when the stress got too much. He'd let me pay him with generous terms. I'd be eternally grateful to him, but he was seriously opinionated about literature.

I went back to my shelving and musing about Ronzo. I hadn't been entirely faking when I got teary about how much I missed him. He'd been away too long. And I hated being in the dark about where he was and how he was doing.

A few minutes later, Orion came running in. At least I thought it was Orion. His beaded dreads had been shorn into a no-nonsense military cut.

"They're back," he said, "The protesters. Only two of them, but Lupe's having a fit. Called the cops. Can I hide out while the po-pos do their thing?"

I had all sorts of questions I'd like to ask him. But I figured I had no business asking a young Black man why he didn't want an encounter with law enforcement. Instead, I asked the other obvious question.

"What happened to your hair? You had such beautiful dreadlocks."

He laughed. "Just part of my act. You sing Rasta music, you need Rasta hair."

"It's extensions?"

He grinned.

A couple of customers came in and started browsing the new arrivals table. They might be actual paying customers, so I went to greet them.

"Can I go hang in Irene's Tarot room?"

I nodded. I had no idea why Orion would want to sit back in that dismal hole, but if it was privacy he wanted, that was the place.

It wasn't until about two hours later, after Felicity came in for her shift, and I took a lunch break, that I realized Orion had left. Not only had he evaporated, but he'd left things a mess. "Irene's room" was even more of a wreck than it had been, with buckets turned upside down and drawers pulled out of the filing cabinet where Felicity stashed the lost hats and sunglasses — and that bedraggled Elmo doll. Which now seemed to be missing.

And I was shocked when I opened the door to my office. The mess was even worse. Papers were scattered everywhere and desk drawers were open.

I needed to have a word with that young man. This was unacceptable. This was another moment when I missed Ronzo.

Felicity knocked and stood in the doorway, breathless. She looked confused as she glanced into the chaos that was my office.

"I don't know what's going on in here, but Lupe wants to talk to you and she's locked and loaded, so be prepared." Felicity stared at the unpaid invoices on the floor.

"Lupe?" I couldn't imagine why my neighbor would be angry with me.

"Yes. Lupe." Lupe herself appeared, pushed past Felicity, then closed the office door in her face. "Not who you were expecting, I bet. Where is he? Under the desk?" She proceeded to bend over and peer under things.

"Excuse me?" was the best response I could come up with.

"You know he's cleaned me out. Emptied the safe." Her words came out in staccato bursts of rage. "I saw him come in here earlier. Before I knew he'd robbed me. But I didn't see him leave. So he must be here."

"Orion? I didn't see him leave either." I took a deep breath. So Orion was a thief. And he'd ripped off his own godmother. I wondered if he'd found anything back here he thought was worth stealing besides the stupid Elmo doll. "He said he wanted to hang out in the utility room Irene uses for her Tarot readings — because you had to call the police on the protesters again."

"You'll have to do better than that. There were no protesters. And I still haven't called the cops. Not about the robbery. I need to talk to that creep first. If he'll return the money and disappear back into the hell he came from, I won't report it. That boy is another tragedy Verline didn't deserve." Lupe leaned down and spoke to the dark space under the desk as if there were any way a six-foot-two man could hide under there. "Did you hear that, you lyin' little jerk?"

Time to calm things down. "Lupe, I know you were fond of Orion, and this is a shock — your own godson stealing your money and betraying your trust. But there's no reason to be angry with me. He seems to have robbed me too. He rummaged through everything. Look at this mess. I don't know if he found anything worth stealing, but it's going to take a lot of time to clean up."

Lupe towered over me and brought her face right down to mine.

"Everybody knows you were sleeping with him, honey. Stop lying."

twenty-five

. . .

Everybody Knows

When Lupe left after her unhinged temper tantrum, I sank into my desk chair and realized I was trembling all over. My hands were so shaky, I couldn't pick up the pencils Orion had dumped from their holder all over the desk. What on earth was happening here?

Lupe said "everybody knows" I'm having an affair with Orion. So who's "everybody"? And why would they make up something so stupid? I admired Orion's good looks, but I wasn't physically attracted to such a young man, any more than I would be sexually attracted to a well-designed pair of shoes.

Who could be making up stories about me? Did I have enemies? The only person I could think of was Dan Fiedler. But what could be his motive? Maybe he thought Ronzo would come out of hiding to defend my honor?

Lupe had left my office door open when she stomped out, so I could hear conversations going on in the store. There were several, and that meant Felicity had her hands full and I needed to get out there and help.

As soon as I sent the customers to the appropriate sections of the store, Felicity grabbed my arm and whispered to me.

"What the hell went on back there? The utility room looks like a tornado hit it and your office is worse."

"Orion," I whispered. "Do not let that young man back into the store. He just robbed Lupe and he may have robbed us too."

"Yes. He took Elmo. At least I didn't see the little red guy in the utility room. I usually have him sitting on top of the lost-and-found filing cabinet."

We heard knocking on the back door. I told Felicity to watch the store and I went to deal with the backdoor visitor. Whatever happened couldn't be much more upsetting than Lupe's visit.

It was Skip. He was holding the Elmo doll. Or what was left of it. Most of the stuffing had been torn out and was scattered all over the patio. If Buckingham had been a younger cat, I could imagine him savaging a toy like that. But Buckingham was too much of a gentleman to do that now, and he didn't tolerate any strays in his territory.

Skip looked almost as disheveled as Elmo. He leaned his bicycle against the side of the building.

"What's going on at the café?" he said. "Does anybody know? I showed up for my shift and nobody's there. She's got the 'closed' sign out front, and the back door is locked. Then I come over here and there's an eviscerated Elmo doll on your steps."

He held out the sad little handful of red plush with big googly eyes on top.

I took it out of politeness, but I had no idea what to do with it.

"So what's up? Do you know what's happened to Lupe?"

I could hear Felicity talking to several people in the store.

"I've got to get back to work, but I'll tell you later. You can rest in my office if you need to. Did you bicycle to work?"

He nodded. "All the way from Los Osos. I try to get here early so I can have a cup of coffee before I start my shift."

"I've got a coffee maker in the office if you're desperate." I patted Skip's shoulder. He followed me and stopped by the open office door.

"What the heck happened in here?"

"Hurricane Orion," I spoke in a low whisper. "He was looking for something. I have no idea what. I don't suppose you'd like to work for me for a couple of hours cleaning up in there? The utility room, too." I indicated the door to the dismal hole. "I'll pay you whatever Lupe does."

"Sure!" Skip lit up with a smile. "I really need the work. Rent is due on Friday."

I handed him back the earthly remains of Elmo. "Come to me if you have any questions." I rushed back into the store. The voices had risen in decibels.

"If you ask me, Lupe's the one that killed that jailbird last month." This came from a large woman I recognized as the hatpin woman who had been so sure Bernard Lanier had been the murderer a few weeks ago. "That nice man with the yacht too."

Poor Felicity stood between the hatpin woman and a man in a cowboy hat I recognized as an occasional customer. He bought used Westerns, mostly. He was a big fan of Louis L'Amour.

"Can I help?" I stood behind the desk and tried to look authoritative. Felicity rolled her eyes and pointed down the hall. I assumed in the direction of the bathroom. I nodded consent.

The hatpin woman and the cowboy were complaining about the closure of the café. I suggested they go to Kat's across the street.

"Kat's is more of a breakfast restaurant, but you can get a good cup of coffee and a muffin over there." I put on my most saccharine smile.

"But they don't have almond brittle. I had my heart set on a pumpkin spice latte and some almond brittle. I've been craving it all morning." The hatpin woman spoke in a grating whine.

"I want to know what's going on," the man said. "I don't like the way they close down a place with no explanation. They don't think about their customers. Why don't you don't sell coffee here? They have coffee at the Barnes and Noble."

I sighed. "Yes, the Barnes and Noble in San Luis is a big store. They have an escalator, too." Another forced smile. "We're just a little place, as you can see. But there are plenty of coffee places in the neighborhood. And Kat's has chocolate chip cookies to die for." I didn't want to have to tell him about Lupe's burglary, since she didn't seem to have reported it yet.

"I don't like that place. Kat's is full of cops," hatpin woman said.

Felicity banged open the back door and came rushing in holding a bag with the Otter Café logo on it.

"Almond brittle!" Her voice was triumphant. "Help yourself. Lupe won't mind. She had to close up because there's been a robbery. The place is a mess."

So much for letting Lupe find Orion before going public with the robbery. I declined the almond brittle. After such a crazy day, I wasn't hungry.

But the contentious visitors were happy to take some. Maybe it would calm them down.

"How did you get in?" I asked Felicity. "Skip said the café was locked up tight."

"Oh, I have a key." She munched down on her own piece of almond brittle.

"Looks like the cops aren't only at Kat's," the man said, after he'd crunched an almond. "They just drove up to Lupe's" He looked through the window and pointed toward the café. "And one looks like he's comin' right here."

"Then I'm out of here. Hate them. Morro Bay cops are a bunch of creeps." Hatpin woman grabbed the man and they both made it out the front door before Officer Pilchard came in.

Felicity offered him some almond brittle, which he declined.

I greeted him with a smile and asked what I could do for him.

He did not smile back.

"What you can do is come down to the station with me, Ms. Randall. We need to question you about a burglary at the Otter Café this morning. We have a witness who says you and your boyfriend, Mr. Orion Jones, took a large amount of cash from the safe at Lupe Sorensen's café."

twenty-six

. . .

Cassoulet

My interrogation by the police was rather silly. At least they were polite. And a little embarrassed. Somebody — probably Lupe — must have fed them a wild story about my life of crime with Orion Jones. Luckily the detective in charge had respect for me as a local business owner, and had a vague recollection of me being famous a long time ago, so she seemed to believe me when I told her I'd been working in my own store all morning, so there wouldn't have been time for me to break into Lupe's safe, even if I'd been so inclined.

Of course I also denied any romantic attachment to young Mr. Jones. I didn't mention that I already had a boyfriend, Ronson Zolek, since Ronzo was probably still on their "persons of interest" list for Boyd Ferrell's murder. They didn't mention either of them, so I felt I'd dodged an awkward moment or two.

Well, actually it was all awkward, since they had been fed such a load of hooey. How could Lupe have done it? Why did she hate me? The whole situation was unfathomable.

When the police dismissed me, I was overjoyed to see Plantagenet waiting for me at the front desk of the police station. It had been less than two hours, but I felt I'd been incarcerated for weeks. I gave Plant a huge bear hug.

"How did you know I was here? It wasn't in the media, was it?" I still had a strong fear of the press after growing up in the spotlight as a famous heiress. Little did they know I'd never inherited anything.

"Oh no. Felicity phoned us." Plant walked me out to his Ferrari, parked in front of the station. "She was terribly worried. She and Skip had to close up the store on their own and she was afraid she wasn't doing things right."

This should have been reassuring, but it wasn't. How did Felicity have Plant and Silas's phone number? It felt weird that she was getting cozy with my friends.

But I shoved that aside. I'd forgotten about poor Skip.

"Skip! Oh, dear. I was going to pay him for the day's work. He needs the money."

"I'm sure he'll survive until tomorrow." Plant opened the car door for me. "Now you're coming to our house for Silas's cassoulet and homemade baguettes."

"But I've got to feed Buckingham." My poor kitty. I hope they'd treated him well and taken him back to the cottage.

"He's had a nice dinner of Fancy Feast seabass and shrimp." Plant gave me a satisfied smile. He was reliably good at taking care of things. "I left him fast asleep on your reading chair."

When we walked into Silas and Plant's elegant house, it was filled with marvelous cooking smells. Silas greeted us with glasses of a hearty old vine zinfandel. I could almost relax.

"Now tell us what's going on." Plant took us into the living room where I sank into a comfy leather chair. He and Silas sat on the couch. "And why didn't you tell us about your new beau, darling? You know we wouldn't have been judgmental about it. After all, Ronzo's been AWOL for some time."

You wouldn't have thought one sip of wine would bring on the waterworks, but I found myself tearing up.

"I wish I knew what's going on. And I certainly don't have a new beau. I've hardly spoken to Orion Jones, and I have no idea why Lupe made up that story. Orion is very good-looking and at first, I thought he might be having a thing with Lupe, but it turned out he's her godson. The son of the dancer named Verline that Boyd Ferrell beat up so badly she could never dance again."

"So is this Orion the one who killed Boyd Ferrell?" Silas jumped in. "That sure is a good motive."

"You're right." I hadn't thought of that, but of course Orion had a motive to kill Boyd. "The only problem is he wasn't there." I sipped wine. "It's pretty tough for a Black person to be invisible in a place like Morro Bay."

"What about Cassius Burgh?" Plant said. "Has he gone underground with Ronzo? We still don't know if he had anything to do with Mr. Ferrell's death, do we?"

"No. We don't know anything. I don't know anything. Except that Ronzo is innocent, and I miss him." I'm afraid I sniffled at that point. "But Ronzo and Cassius certainly can't be accused of taking part in Bernard's murder, so I wish the police would take them off their list, now that they've got two bodies."

"Are you sure the murders are connected?" Silas said. "Maybe Bernard was killed by a jealous lover, or more likely, somebody after those diamonds."

A timer dinged and he rushed off to the kitchen.

"Silas is making a lot of sense." Plant could be infuriatingly logical. "The two men didn't have much common history, and they certainly moved in different circles."

"Well, I keep thinking Lupe must have killed Boyd, but she didn't have a motive to kill Bernard, unless it was to steal his diamonds." I had to voice my growing suspicion of Lupe. At this point I could believe she was capable of anything. "But she doesn't know anything about sailing, so she would have needed an accomplice who's a seasoned sailor to get that yacht out of Morro Bay harbor. Skip says that's a 'gnarly' spot, squeezing between Morro Rock and the breakwater."

"Oh really?" Plant perked up. "Skip is an experienced sailor? Do you think he might have been having a thing with Bernard. Maybe Bernard was Skip's sugar daddy?"

I laughed. "The only trouble with that theory is it looks as if

Bernard didn't actually have much money. And what little he had, he used to help Irene."

"But he had a yacht. That must have looked pretty good to Skip if he's a sailor." Plant gave me a dark look. "Don't underestimate that kid."

"Yes, Skip could have killed him. I guess you have a point." I sipped wine and pondered for a moment.

"Okay, let's say the murders were entirely separate. Lupe killed Boyd to avenge the long-ago attack on her friend, and Skip killed Bernard hoping to get his yacht and maybe the diamonds. I haven't heard anything about Bernard's will. I wonder if he left the *Mary Sue* to Skip. Although apparently it wasn't his anyway."

"And of course the diamonds weren't either." Plant finished off his wine.

"And then there's your mysterious friend Dan Fiedler." Silas emerged from the kitchen. "I think that guy has nefarious motives. He's always asking inappropriate questions. And we can never be sure of our Felicity. She might have done them in with daggers of almond brittle." He laughed and made a dramatic gesture toward the dining room. "Ladies and gentlemen, dinner is served."

The cassoulet smelled heavenly and tasted even better. For a moment we were silent, appreciating the duck, lamb, pork hocks and sausage all simmered with vegetables, herbs, and cannellini beans. Silas must have been working on it for days. I made appreciative sounds, while thinking that the jumble of suspects in our mysterious deaths was rather like this dish — impossible to isolate one taste from the other, while they all made one formidable pot of stew.

twenty-seven

. . .

Fun With Elmo

The next morning, I was relieved to see Lupe's café open and full of customers. Maybe things would go back to normal. I was sad for her, of course, It was awful that Orion had turned out to be such a creep and she'd lost all that money. What made her so deluded about me and Orion was still a mystery, but I was going to try to put it down to the trauma of being burgled. Small businesses worked with a very slim profit margin in Morro Bay these days, so she was facing some financial anxiety. But her business was popular, and I was sure she'd make up the money soon.

But it would take longer to get over the fact her godson betrayed her trust. It was such a tragedy that he had so little love or respect for a woman who obviously adored him. No matter what I thought of her, she didn't deserve that. And if she had killed Boyd Ferrell, it would have been to avenge Boyd's attack on Orion's mother Verline, so his betrayal would have been especially wounding.

And I still had to assess the damage Orion had done to me. Skip had done a fine job tidying up the mess Orion had made. Skip had left the eviscerated Elmo neatly laid out on my desk. It belonged in the trash, but somehow, I couldn't throw it out. It had been in the lost-and-found for months, so I'm sure whatever tourist's child had lost it was long gone. But maybe it could be salvaged. Some seamstress could use quilt batting to restore the doll to its former squishiness.

Except I didn't know any seamstresses. I was wasting time. I had to open up the store in a few minutes. I realized I'd been putting off looking in the safe to see if Orion had cleaned me out, too. But when I opened it, I saw everything was intact. Even the old Christmas gift bag filled with Raccoon Alice's crystals and Tarot decks. Ronzo had tossed the bag in the safe until he had time to look at them properly. Now, I knew I should choose the inventory myself or give the samples back to Alice.

Buckingham was snaking around my legs in a needy way to let me know my presence had been missed last night when I slept in Plant and Silas's guest room. I didn't have time to pick him up and give him the cuddles he'd missed. I felt guilty that I'd left him on his own when Orion might be planning to sneak back and steal what he couldn't find the first time. I didn't know that Orion would hurt my kitty, but I honestly didn't know anything about the man at this point.

Except I did know he tore apart a child's toy for no apparent reason. He had to be harboring a lot of anger, and angry men were dangerous.

The day went by pretty smoothly, although I kept jumping at every sound, scared that Orion would reappear. Or that I'd have to deal with Lupe's bizarre accusations again. But I only had a trickle of quiet customers. Nobody mentioned my visit to the police station, so I assumed it hadn't caught the attention of anybody in the neighboring businesses. In fact, I almost forgot about the incident myself until Felicity showed up for her shift and wanted me to "spill the tea."

As annoying as she was, I was glad for her company. My jitters calmed down. Although she reminded me that Lupe could still be a threat.

"That woman is totally delulu," Felicity said, making circles around her ear with an index finger. "How could she think Orion was your boyfriend? You're over forty!"

Felicity had a gift for saying exactly the wrong thing. Or maybe the right thing if she wanted me to feel bad. And she was on a roll.

"Not that I blame Lupe for thinking you might move on from that

Ronzo guy, it's so obvious he isn't coming back. He doesn't even text you? It's time to get real, Camilla."

I "got real" by going back to the office and going over my order for new books. I needed mindless paperwork to keep me from thinking about how Felicity might be right. There had been no news about the investigation into Boyd Ferrell's death for weeks, and we didn't even know for sure that Ronzo was still a "person of interest." He could at least have sent me a text saying that he was okay. Or that he thought about me once in a while. If only the police would zero in on Lupe. She certainly had a motive to kill Boyd, and I could believe her enthusiasm for seeing him had been fake. She had been close enough to him that night to slip a stiletto into his *medulla oblongata* and I wouldn't be at all surprised to find out she had such a weapon, given her history with underworld types in her days as a showgirl.

I had to leave the sanctuary of my office when traffic picked up in late afternoon, and I could keep busy gift-wrapping coffee table books and finding obscure science fiction titles for pimply teenaged boys.

Then Gloria, the dress shop owner in black, swooped in to chastise me for not carrying Tarot cards and crystals.

"Don't blame me when you go out of business," she said, wafting her black scarf. "I've sent two of my customers over here to buy New Age material and all they could find was a book by Deepak Chopra and a bunch of stuff from Marianne Williamson. Not everybody wants books."

No. Not everybody wanted books. A bookstore had to carry other things these days. It was probably time for me to make a decision about buying inventory from Raccoon Alice.

In late afternoon, Felicity asked if she could get off early and I was happy to let her go. She was a good, organized worker. I shouldn't have let her negativity get to me. I was probably on overload. I looked forward to an evening of cuddling up with a good book and my cat.

But when I locked up the store and went out to the courtyard, I could see something was wrong. Buckingham wasn't in his usual spot in front of the cottage door waiting to be let in. In fact, he didn't even come when I called him. This was his dinner time, and he was always eager for food.

Then I went to the door and put the key in the lock, but it was already unlocked. Chills gripped me. Had Orion somehow got inside my home? What did he want from me?

"Buckingham?" I called as I opened the door.

"He's in here, having a little fun with Elmo," a man's voice said.

There in the living room, was Dan Fiedler, sitting on my couch, watching my cat attack what was left of Elmo.

twenty-eight

. . .

Investigations

Trying to hide my shaking hands, I decided to act as if finding an intruder in my living room playing with my cat was perfectly normal. I offered to make Dan some tea, but he declined. He also declined to tell me why he was in my house. He said he'd found the key in the obvious place — under the geranium pot. Then he'd seen Elmo's remains and thought it was a cat toy, so he'd given the red plush thing to Buckingham.

But he didn't tell me what the hell he was doing here. Was he being friendly, or was he here to terrorize me — or worse?

He was wearing his Friends of the Library tee-shirt again. Maybe he had a bunch of them. They did make him seem less dangerous somehow.

I sank into my chair, feeling betrayed by my cat and furious at Dan's invasion of my space. If he'd snatched Elmo, he'd been in my office, too. If he was just being friendly, why not come talk to me in the store? I didn't know if I should be afraid of him or simply annoyed. He wasn't young and buffed like Orion, but he was fit and could probably do me damage if he wanted to.

"Dan, what's going on? Are you stalking me, or what? Why are you being so weird?"

"Am I weird?" Dan spoke more to Buckingham than to me. "I'm looking for some things, Camilla, and I think you know where they are. Ronzo told me I should never underestimate you."

"Ronzo? You've talked to Ronzo?" This was probably another of Dan's ploys to get me to reveal where Ronzo was hiding.

"I had some business in New Jersey. I was able to have a quick conversation with him."

"He's all right?" This certainly was welcome information, even when delivered in such a creepy way. "Do you know for sure whether he's still a person of interest with the local police?"

"The Bozos in the Morro Bay P.D. don't have a clue. I think it's obvious who killed Ferrell, but they won't figure it out. Unless somebody confesses, they're going to keep looking at Ronson Zolek. And apparently he's going to keep staying undercover with those gangster cousins of his."

"So he is with those cousins? I was afraid of that. They're scary people. I don't think they're in any sort of gang, but they act like gangsters."

"Oh, they're in some kind of gang all right. The Balkan mafia is still very much in control of a lot of the smuggling into North Jersey. They've teamed up with the DeCavalcante family and you don't want to cross them."

"My goodness. You're awfully well versed in the crime doings in New Jersey. Did you live there?" I wanted a glass of wine. But then I'd have to offer Dan some, and he'd get comfortable and not leave.

"I went to college in New Jersey," he said. "Rutgers. Then I joined the FBI."

This hit my brain with a thud. "You're an FBI agent? I thought you worked in insurance. Am I being investigated? By the FBI?" I did not like where this was going. What had Ronzo got mixed up in?

"No. I'm retired." Dan laughed. "I'm a private investigator now."

Buckingham had jumped on his lap and was purring away while Dan petted him. I felt like throwing them both out of my house.

"And now you're investigating Ronzo? And me?"

"Not really. I'm trying to find some diamonds. For an insurance company. For a while I thought your friend Ronzo might have stolen them that night Boyd Ferrell died. Ronzo does have a shady past and some mob connections. But now I'm pretty sure he doesn't have them."

He suspected Ronzo of being a thief? That was probably why he'd been trying to find out where Ronzo was. I tried to maintain my polite smile.

"So you're a private detective looking for the diamonds that Bernard stole? That's why you've been cozying up to all of Bernard's friends?" This was quite a revelation. "But why do you think I know where Bernard's diamonds are? Do you think Ronzo stole them and gave them to me for safe-keeping?"

"No. I'm pretty sure now that Ronzo didn't take them. And please — they were never Bernard's diamonds. They belong to a man named Eugene Delacorte, a resident of Louisiana. He hired me because he knew Bernard was headed this way with the *Mary Sue*. Which also belongs to Mr. Delacorte, by the way. But the diamonds aren't onboard. The police have scoured the vessel since Bernard died."

"Who do you think killed Bernard? They can't exactly blame Ronzo for that." I really needed some wine. "Would you like a glass of chardonnay? I have some in the fridge." I went to the kitchen for the bottle and two glasses.

"Sure." Dan laughed. "But don't worry. Even the local Bozos don't think your boyfriend has teleporting powers. I don't know who's on their suspect list for Bernard's murder — if it was murder — but my money is on Orion Jones. He's an experienced sailor, it turns out. Spent some time on a fishing boat out of Kingston. And he's definitely after the diamonds. He not only ransacked your store and Lupe's, but he also broke into Skip's little beach hovel in Los Osos, and Alice Rafferty's house in Pismo Beach."

"Raccoon Alice? She got ransacked, too?" I poured Dan some wine.

"Yes. The day before you and Lupe were hit. It's where Irene has been staying. He must have thought Bernard gave the diamonds to Irene for safe keeping. But I think Bernard realized Irene isn't all that reliable."

"But I'm reliable, so he supposedly gave me the diamonds?" I took a sip of wine. It didn't help much.

Dan sat back and gave me a big grin.

"That was my theory. Of all the people Bernard hung out with in Morro Bay, you seem the most stable."

Stable. Oh, dear. Not only over forty, but stable. Not exactly flattering. But things were starting to make a little sense, except the fact that Dan thought I had the stupid diamonds.

I took another sip. "I wish I could help you. I really do. I certainly don't want any stolen diamonds. I had to sell most of the family jewelry when my mother died with overwhelming debts, but I don't miss it at all. Of course Mr. Delacorte deserves to be reunited with his property. But I do not have a clue where it could be. I've never seen these diamonds. I'd never even heard about them until after Bernard's demise."

"Who told you about them?"

"Plantagenet. I already told you that. He heard rumors about Bernard's stolen diamonds in a gay bar in West Hollywood."

"So he tells me."

The man was shameless. He had questioned everybody I knew, it seemed. But no matter how many people he talked to, he wasn't going to make me know what I didn't know.

I leaned forward and looked him in the eye.

"Who told you I had the diamonds? Was it Orion Jones? At least now I know why he tore up my office and store room. And took all the stuffing out of Elmo. I thought that was insane, but maybe he thought I'd sewed some diamonds in there."

Dan gave a big laugh and picked up Elmo from the floor.

"He just might have. Except these rocks are big. They're uncut. Bigger than golf balls. This little Elmo would have looked awfully chunky." He wiggled the Elmo in front of Buckingham as the cat purred on his lap.

I felt a little better knowing Dan wasn't some assassin or criminal, but I still didn't want him in my living room. Especially since I still found him rather attractive. I had to put on my best Manners Doctor persona. I stood up.

"Don't feel you have to stay," I said. "Buckingham needs his dinner and I need a little time to decompress after a stressful day."

He lifted Buckingham gently and put him on the floor.

"Of course. But here's my card. If you have any leads about the diamonds, do phone me." He handed me a business card. "Fiedler Investigations" it said. There was a line drawing of a magnifying glass. Not exactly original.

"I promise," I said. "I'd say I'll search my entire store and cottage, but I think Orion beat me to it. I don't suppose you know where he is?"

"Probably long gone. He has been a suspect in thefts everywhere he travels. He's been on his own since he ran away from foster care when he was sixteen and he seems to have run from trouble to trouble ever since."

"But he had a record deal! At least that's what Felicity told me."

"He does have a recording contract with Pacific Records, but I don't know how much money a musician actually makes these days. Ten out of every eleven albums lose money. Whatever money they gave him on signing wouldn't be enough to live on. Certainly not enough to make him change his thieving ways."

That was interesting information. I wondered if Lupe had found out about her godson's criminal past. I walked to the door and opened it. At least I didn't have to be afraid of Dan anymore. He did have a lovely smile. And he was good at ferreting out information.

"I'll phone you if I hear anything." I clutched his business card. Fiedler Investigations. If only I were rich enough to hire him to find out who really killed Boyd Ferrell.

twenty-nine

• • •

A Bad Time for Scorpios

When she arrived for her shift the next day, Felicity was in one of her moods. I couldn't tell if she had some issue with me, or if she was angry with the world in general. When I asked her how her day was going, she was her usual whiny self.

"Probably not as good as yours. You're so oblivious to everything, you can go through life pretending to be happy. I can't. You have no idea. What made you decide to give Elmo to your cat to destroy? I thought I was in charge of the lost-and-found."

I tried to explain to her about finding Elmo with the stuffing pulled out after Orion's rampage, and how Dan Fiedler thought it was a cat toy and gave it to Buckingham.

"Dan Fiedler. Yeah. I saw his car parked around the corner last night. I guess he didn't want anybody to know you two are doing it again."

Thank goodness we had no customers in the store. The last thing I needed was people spreading a ridiculous rumor about me and Dan Fiedler.

"Mr. Fiedler and I are not 'doing' anything. And we never have. I have a boyfriend." I tried to keep the anger out of my voice. "Dan came by to tell me he'd got hold of Ronzo and he's still staying with his cousins in Newark."

"Oh, Dan Fiedler is buddies with Ronzo now? When did that happen?" She had a particular tone she used when she wanted to imply I was lying. I prayed Ronzo would be able to come back soon. I didn't know how much longer I could put up with this. I reminded myself she was temporary "help," and I could let her go as soon as Ronzo showed up.

I gave her a bland smile. "I have no idea when they became friends. Probably when Ronzo worked here. Why don't you do some clean-up in the Horror section? Some kids were in there earlier and got the titles all mixed up."

Felicity's facial expression changed from hostile to fake concern as she put a hand on my arm.

"Camilla, be careful. Dan is bad news. He's a private detective, you know. He's only hanging around because he thinks you know where the diamonds are."

So Felicity knew who Dan was. I wondered how long she'd known. Everybody seemed to know more than I did.

And did any of them care who really killed Boyd Ferrell? Everybody was interested in those diamonds, but I couldn't see that Boyd had anything to do with them, or with Bernard Lanier, or secret gay trysts at Pirate's Cove or any of those other mysterious goings-on.

Was anybody even trying to find Boyd's killer? Did everybody assume Ronzo was guilty? Maybe I really should hire Dan Fiedler. As if I could afford him.

"Oh, Camilla, I think you need a reading." I looked up and there was Irene, with more scarves and jangly jewelry than ever. "This is a bad time for Scorpios, you know. And I'm sure you're feeling the effects of Mercury retrograde."

"I think I'll weather the storm." I gave her a Manners Doctor smile. I suppose I'd told her I had a birthday coming up, and she'd figured out I'm a Scorpio.

"A reading will help. You're in danger, Camilla. I can feel it. Can we go to your back room?"

I told her about our Orion attack and how the room had been trashed.

"How about we go to your office?" She looked around the store. "You don't seem to have any customers. I'm sure Felicity can hold the fort while you get a quick reading?" She directed the last comment at the Horror section, where Felicity was tidying things up as asked.

"That's fine," Felicity said. "Why are all these Colleen Hoover romances in Horror?"

"College kids," was all I could say while Irene grabbed my arm and pulled me back to my office.

I tried not to fidget while Irene held me hostage as she spread her silk scarf on my desk and went through her ritual shuffling and cutting of cards. She spoke some New Age babble about lunar nodes in Chiron and retrograde planets, as she placed the cards in a cross pattern. She scrutinized them, shaking her head.

"It's worse than I thought," she said. "Swords. Look at all those swords. Just like before. You remember that one means betrayal. It's in your recent past. Somebody close to you has betrayed you." She pointed to that same old nasty card showing a man face down with ten swords stuck in his back. "You've been stabbed in the back. And look there, In the future. That's you, crying."

She pointed at a card showing a woman weeping on a bed, with nine swords hung on the wall behind her — that "Lord of Cruelty" card. These cards needed a new theme.

"Cruelty again. That's the treachery card. You need to protect your-self, Camilla. Someone is going to break your heart."

I knew Irene imagined she was being kind, but I felt as if she'd been sticking those swords in me and was trying to finish me off with blows about the head.

She could tell I was upset. "You know what, honey? Maybe this reading isn't accurate because I didn't have a crystal. I remember my client Tina wanted crystals to clarify her reading last time." She gathered the cards together again. "I don't suppose you're carrying any crystals in the store yet?"

"No. I wanted Ronzo to make that decision, but..." I remembered

Raccoon Alice's crystal samples. "I have the samples Alice gave us. They're in the safe. Shall I get them?"

Irene nodded as she chanted something and re-shuffled the cards.

I got Alice's well-worn Christmas gift bag out of the safe. Inside were several Tarot decks, plus a brown cardboard box and a bigger, more elegant box with compartments for each crystal. I opened the brown box and poured the crystals onto Irene's scarf. I was surprised they were so large. They definitely wouldn't work in the store.

"Do you want to choose one?" I offered.

Irene glanced at them. "Not the big ugly ones. Bernard just picked them up on Moonstone beach. No. In the other box there's some lovely pieces of rose quartz. Rose quartz is a healing crystal. It symbolizes unconditional love. I'll do a simple three-card spread. I'm sure it will be more positive."

I put the other crystals back in the box while she dealt three cards. They were the nine and ten of swords, and another showing a heart with three swords piercing it.

"Oh, dear," Irene said. "Your readings certainly are consistent: heartbreak, treachery, and betrayal." She handed me the rose quartz crystal as she put the cards back in the deck. "Well, I told you it's a bad time for Scorpios."

thirty

. . .

The Grapes of Wrath

After I put Alice's crystals back in the safe, I heard conversation coming from the store. I wanted some time to cheer myself up after Irene's consistently awful Tarot readings, but I needed to go out to help Felicity. She wasn't always up to date on bestsellers, and she didn't know a thing about classic literature. Out on the floor, a man's booming voice was holding forth on the importance of John Steinbeck and the *Grapes of Wrath*. Felicity responded that she liked Henry Fonda, but we didn't carry DVDs.

"Everybody uses streaming apps now," she said in her condescending whine.

I rushed in and gave the man a big smile.

"You're looking for the Literature section." I swept him down the aisle to where we shelved our classics. "We have *The Grapes of Wrath* in a collectible hardcover edition as well as the paperback."

He seemed willing to ignore Felicity's cluelessness. He said he was driving up to the Steinbeck Museum in Salinas in a couple of days and wanted to reread the book.

When I got back to the desk, Felicity was on the store's landline phone.

"It's for you." She handed me the receiver. "Some lady with a phony English accent. Sounds kinda bananas." She sauntered off to the back room, carrying a pair of sunglasses that had been sitting on the remainder table since yesterday. Another addition to her lost-and-found department.

The person on the phone was Vera, office manager at Sherwood Ltd, the British company that published my etiquette books. Vera's Midlands accent didn't sound exactly like BBC English, which is why it might have sounded "phony" to Felicity.

"Pradeep wants you to know he's been in touch with Seattle and had a proper chin wag." Vera did sound a bit agitated. "He's going to get it sorted."

"Seattle? Pradeep is coming to Seattle?" Pradeep Balasubramarian had taken over as the director of the company while the owner, Peter Sherwood, was off adventuring.

"Oh my, no. He's simply been on the blower with some people at Amazon headquarters. About your dodgy book reviews."

"Reviews say my etiquette books are dodgy?" I hadn't looked at any of my book pages on Amazon for months. I had so few sales these days, and the reviews were all from years ago.

"The new ones. Yes. They're ridiculous. Nobody who's read *Good Manners for Bad Times* would call you an ignorant slut or a gangster's ho, whatever that means. I can't imagine a gangster using a gardening implement." Vera gave an audible sigh. "I certainly hope they'll take them down immediately. If your books don't sell, Amazon doesn't make money either."

"An ignorant slut? A gangster's ho? Somebody wrote that about me in an Amazon review?" I'd swear a little creature with a hammer was inside my head, pounding away. This made even less sense than Irene's Tarot readings.

"Oh, yes. They've written those things in a lot of Amazon reviews — and worse. At least fifty of them, last count. New ones keep coming in. Pradeep's a wreck. And now Peter's weighing in. He's alive and well in New Zealand, by the way. He thinks this nonsense is coming from one of his enemies in Australian organized crime. But I don't think this slander is aimed at Sherwood. I find it obvious that you're the target. I don't suppose you've got the foggiest who wrote them?"

"How long has this been going on?" I had to sit down. My head wouldn't stop spinning. Anonymous hate was so disconcerting. Could this be one of Ronzo's enemies? Something triggered by Dan Fiedler's investigations? Maybe it was the crazed anti-vaxxers, who knew I was a friend of Lupe's.

"The first ones appeared a few weeks ago on Amazon's US site. A few unpleasant one-stars. And now Amazon shows them on the UK site as well. They keep coming every few days — each one barmier than the last."

"So this is an American who's after me?" I looked around for Felicity. I needed to take a break to process this. But she seemed to be taking her time in the lost-and-found department.

"I'd say so. But Peter believes otherwise. Thank goodness you haven't seen them. Don't. Stay off Amazon, and Pradeep should have them taken down in a day or two."

"Can he do that? I thought Amazon never took down reviews." My coffee was cold. I needed a fresh cup. Or even better, a glass of wine.

"If he can't, Peter will. And cause an international incident, I shouldn't wonder. You know how he is."

Yes, I knew how Peter Sherwood was. He believed laws didn't apply to him. I had to hope Pradeep had the power to convince the people in Seattle. I assured Vera that I'd be in touch if I discovered where the reviews were coming from.

But I didn't have a clue. I felt frozen, as if I were in a nightmare, unable to wake up. Maybe I really was the man in Irene's Tarot card picture, with a bunch of swords stuck in my back.

I slowly became aware that the Steinbeck man was standing at the desk with his paperback copy of the *Grapes of Wrath*, waiting for me to ring it up. He looked down on me as if I were some species of insect.

"Are you going to be able to ring this up for me any time soon?"

Felicity appeared at his side.

"I can do that for you." She took the book and came behind the desk and pushed me aside as I stood to help.

"I'll be, um, taking a break." I could feel my face burning. What was wrong with me? I started toward my office and then went straight out the back door to my cottage.

It wasn't until I got to my front door that I realized Buckingham had been trotting behind me. He must have thought it was closing time. And cat-feeding time. He gave a plaintive meow.

After I fed him, I tried to pull myself together. These stupid reviews weren't the end of the world. I reminded myself I wasn't counting on my royalties to pay my bills anymore. Still, I needed to deal with this whole thing. I took out my phone and called Plantagenet.

"Darling, I don't want to get caught in the middle of this," he said as soon as he picked up the phone.

"The middle of what?" His tone was odd. Exasperated.

"If you've got a problem with Felicity, address it directly to her. Shaming her in front of a customer isn't exactly worthy of the Manners Doctor, is it?"

"Felicity? Felicity has been talking to you?" What was up with that woman? Didn't she have friends of her own? Why did she need to co-opt mine?

"Oh, yes. She just hung up. She calls me all the time to complain about you. You've got to get her to stop. It's interrupting my work, and driving Silas crazy."

"But that's awful. Why would she do that? I didn't shame her in front of any customers."

"You didn't make fun of her for not knowing *The Grapes of Wrath* was a book as well as a movie?"

"I didn't shame her. I simply helped the customer."

"Well, you two need to work it out. She felt disrespected. Listen, darling. I need to get off the phone —"

"Don't hang up. That's not why I called. Do you know about my Amazon reviews?"

"Oh, have you got some bad reviews? Welcome to my world, darling. All writers get rotten reviews. It's a rite of passage. Do you remember what *The New Yorker* said about my *Wilde in the West*? And it went on to get an Oscar. If you need cheering up, go read some Amazon reviews of classics. They're hilarious."

"This isn't ordinary reviews. It's —"

He hung up on me. This really was a swords-in-the-back kind of day.

Maybe I should take his advice. I booted up my laptop and went to Amazon. I was tempted to look at the review fiasco, but instead, I searched for the *Grapes of Wrath* and clicked on its one-star reviews.

"I'm thirteen years old and this is the most boringest book in my whole live," said the first one.

"The only interesting part is when a guy kills a guy after another guy kills a guy, but that lasted about a page," said another.

And then: "I like pickles. They are my favorite candy." That was the entire review.

I felt a deep laugh coming from my belly. I laughed until tears ran down my cheeks. Buckingham came over to my chair and gave me a concerned look.

I scooped him up and giggled into his soft fur. It was funny. My anger deflated. I would have to trample my wrathful grapes another day. All I needed was for Ronzo to come home so I could fire Felicity. And that wouldn't happen until he was no longer a suspect in Boyd Ferrell's murder. But it looked as if nobody wanted to solve the mystery but me.

thirty-one

. . .

Google is Our Friend

When Ronzo was doing his detective work, he'd always start with the computer. "Google is our friend," he'd say in a silly preschool teacher voice.

So I decided I should start my search for Boyd Ferrell's killer with some Googling. Buckingham seemed to approve. He was purring away on the desk next to my laptop.

First, I needed a list of suspects. Lots of people disliked Boyd, because of his violent past, but who might have actually killed him? If I looked at it honestly, the person who had the best motive was Orion Jones. Boyd had crippled his mother and sent her to an early grave, which threw him into the foster care system and a life of crime.

Big problem: he wasn't there. I knew that for certain. Unfortunately, Morro Bay was not a diverse town. A Black man would be noticeable anywhere. And the only Black man at the Moth event was Cassius Burgh. Who left for Fisherman Jack's before the murder.

So I should forget motives for the moment and look at people who had opportunity. Lupe was at the top of my list right now. She'd been flitting around the crowd all that evening, getting very close to Boyd, hugging him on several occasions.

Then I had to look at Skip, since he was standing behind Boyd right around the time it happened.

And I couldn't leave out the mysterious thief, Bernard, who had been alive and kicking when Boyd died.

And I guess I could still include Cassius Burgh. He might have sneaked back from Jack's when nobody was looking. Was he not a person of interest anymore, but Ronzo was? I wished I could just march into the Morro Bay Police Department and ask, but they'd try to get me to tell them where Ronzo was. Which I genuinely did not know. So they'd treat me as a useless flake again.

I had to include Dan Fiedler. The fact he'd turned out to be a private detective didn't really remove him from the list. Now that I'd seen the menace under his Friend of the Library persona, I couldn't unsee it.

Irene had been hanging around Boyd that night, too, along with Raccoon Alice. And there was Felicity, of course, but she was mostly behind the muffin-selling table. And of course she had no motive. Actually, neither did Irene or Alice. Unless Alice mistook Boyd for a raccoon.

Buckingham gave a big yawn. Obviously he didn't approve of my joke, even though I didn't say it out loud.

So, all these people had opportunity. But who had motive? Lupe had a strong one, which was that Boyd gave her friend Verline that life-destroying beating back in New Jersey. She might have invited Boyd to the Moth event because she wanted to do him harm, instead of rekindle an old flame as she first said.

Skip had the best opportunity, but he didn't have much of a motive, unless it had something to do with his secret affair with Bernard, and those elusive diamonds. So I couldn't rule him out completely.

And what about Bernard himself? He had opportunity, but as to motive, I suppose all those people could be right that Boyd's Moth story was about Bernard. Although I thought that was pretty far-fetched. Boyd wouldn't be stupid enough to tell a story about a dead woman being tossed off a yacht if the tosser was present. But Bernard certainly was the shadiest person on the list after Orion. In fact, I guess he wasn't even Bernard. What had Plant said? He'd used names like

Lucky Lanier, Bernie Lane, and Boniface LeBlanc. So Mr. Pseudonym made number two on my list after Lupe.

Then I needed to investigate Cassius Burgh. Ronzo had trusted him enough to leave everything he had here, and go off to New York with him, but who was he, really?

Then there was Dan Fiedler. I should look into his background. He was certainly at the event, talking to Boyd. I had no idea if he had a motive, but he might have had a connection to that casino where Boyd had worked.

"Okay, Bucky. We're going to do some Googling on these five. They're my top suspects." Buckingham looked up at me, then closed his eyes. I guess he thought that sounded boring.

It wasn't boring, but it was predictable. Guadalupe Ingrid Sorensen was born in Solvang, the Danish town about an hour and a half drive south of Morro Bay. Mother Mexican and father Danish. That made sense — with her Valkyrie height and all that dark Mexican hair. She was fifty-six years old. Had been divorced once, from a man named Mace O'Rourke of Atlantic City, since deceased. She had two tickets for speeding in Nevada, and an arrest for assaulting a man in Las Vegas twenty years ago, by lifting him over her head and threatening to throw him down some stairs. But she didn't seem to have been sent to jail. I could imagine she might do an overhead press with some drunken lout who'd made a rude pass at her. I'd seen her sling those huge sacks of flour around. The story had made the *Las Vegas Review-Journal*, probably because it was accompanied by a photo of her in all her showgirl finery. She had been even more stunning at thirty-six.

I guess if she'd injured a rude casino customer, she might be capable of lethally attacking Boyd Ferrell, but her Las Vegas escapade sounded more like a demonstration of strength than an assault. And she hadn't had as much as a parking ticket in ten years. She had over a thousand friends on Facebook, and mostly seemed to post photos of the café and its award-winning muffins and almond brittle. Her X-Twitter account was set to private — probably because of those lunatic anti-vaxxers — and she didn't seem to be on Instagram or TikTok.

Skip, whose name Felicity had told me was Stanley Irving, was twenty-six, born in San Luis Obispo and a graduate of Morro Bay High

School. He'd been on the winning soccer team his freshman year. Two years ago, he'd appeared in a community theater production of *Guys and Dolls* as Nicely Nicely Johnson. He didn't seem to be on social media at all. He sang in the choir of the Methodist church. Kind of a model citizen.

Then I tackled Bernard. I found dozens of stories about his naked body being found at Pirate's Cove, but almost nothing before that. He must have only been using that name for a short time. He was my most sinister suspect, but I couldn't find out anything about him. I tried "Lucky Lanier" and the other names I could remember, but came up with nothing but an obituary for Boniface LeBlanc, who died in 1952 in Louisiana, following a knife fight in a New Orleans bar.

I found lots of information on Cassius Burgh, but it was all stories about promotional events for Pacific Records. He seemed to have been born in Oakland and went to public schools there, where he had been on the honor roll. He got a degree in business from UCLA and he was forty-eight. No social media accounts. I couldn't even find a motor vehicle violation.

Then I went looking for Daniel Fiedler. There were hundreds of them. Thousands. Most of the Daniel Fiedlers on the first Google pages seemed to be lawyers. A couple were accountants. One was an evangelical preacher. I finally found Daniel Fiedler, private investigator, in a recent Yelp entry on page ten. He got four stars from somebody who said he'd found their missing French bulldog. "Dan's language can get a little salty" the customer said. "That cost him one star. But I'm glad he volunteers at the library."

Not one of these people looked like a potential murderer. This wasn't working. I didn't have Ronzo's skills in knowing where to look and what to look for. It would probably be pointless to go on to Google Irene, Alice, and Felicity. Besides, it was late and I needed to go to bed.

"And so, Buckingham," I told the sleeping cat. "We have what my ex-husband would call bupkis. Nothing. Nada. I guess Google is not our friend after all."

thirty-two

. . .

I Feel So Break-Up

I was getting tired of tiptoeing around Felicity. I didn't know why she was taking offense at everything I said, but it was getting annoying. And it was even more annoying that she was co-opting my best friend to complain about my so-called transgressions. I was afraid to even phone Plant these days, since I'd get an earful about what awful thing Felicity imagined I'd done to her that day.

"She doesn't like you to use the word 'need' because it shows how needy you are." Plant had told me. "She finds that offensive. Instead of saying 'I'll need you to do some shelving today,' say 'your task today is shelving,' or something like that."

"I'm supposed to say, 'your task today is…' What am I — a robot? A Martha from *A Handmaid's Tale*? That's insane."

Then Plant would refuse to talk about it and tell me I had to stop her from taking up his time. We'd been best friends for nearly twenty-five years, but Felicity had managed to erode that friendship in a matter of weeks.

I also had to avoid Lupe. She still seemed to believe I'd had some sort of liaison with her godson. If Orion was her godson at all. After what Dan Fiedler told me about his criminal past, I wondered if

Verline had really been Orion's mother, or whether Mr. Fake Dread-locks had made the whole thing up just to con Lupe.

The one thing I knew was that he had evaporated after our Morro Bay robberies. There was no news that he'd been arrested. Even though he'd ransacked Skip's place in Los Osos, too, and Raccoon Alice's Pismo Beach house, so there had to be police and sheriff's deputies from those towns looking for him too. Unless maybe breaking into houses and stores wasn't a big enough crime to keep the attention of local law enforcement. Anyway, I wasn't sure Orion had stolen items of value from anybody but Lupe. In any case, nobody seemed to have heard from him since the day he broke into the safe at the Otter Café and then came here and gutted our lost-and-found Elmo doll.

I was glad he'd disappeared. It would have been awfully difficult to be polite to him after all that.

Felicity had moped around about him for a few days. Like a lot of Lupe's customers, she missed Orion's music. Lupe had of course needed to replace him for performances over the weekend. She'd called in a local singer-songwriter who sang sad songs about climate change, which didn't go over as well as Orion's catchy Caribbean tunes.

"I sure liked that good-looking Rasta guy better," one of my customers said on Monday afternoon. "I loved the way he sang that Beach Boys song about the Sloop John B. He made it sound almost like a real Caribbean folk song."

"I loved how he sang that," another woman chimed in. She started to sing. "I feel so break-up, I wanna go home."

Of course I couldn't tell them it was indeed a real Caribbean folk song — and the Beach Boys had merely covered it. Felicity would have talked Plant's ear off about my "disrespect" of customers.

I pretty much had to keep silent when she was around. And I couldn't be sure my memory was right about the song, anyway. I was questioning everything these days. Especially my own sanity. My pens kept disappearing. And my coffee cup was constantly wandering. My Manners Doctor books kept disappearing from the shelves too, even though there was no record of any sales. I knew retail theft was getting worse, but why steal etiquette books, when there were bestsellers all over the place?

I had no idea. I didn't have many ideas these days.

And then there were the reviews. Pradeep had managed to get the most toxic ones taken down, so there were no more *ad hominem* attacks calling me a gangster's ho or an ignorant slut, but several scathing one-stars were left that kept my rating at two stars. My Amazon sales had stopped dead.

I needed some time off. And I needed Ronzo. I hated the fact that nobody seemed to be in touch with him but the enigmatic Dan Fiedler. But Dan was pretty much the only person I could talk to these days. Well, except for Buckingham. In fact, if it weren't for Buckingham, I might have simply closed up the store and gone to New Jersey myself to try to find Ronzo. I did have addresses for two of his cousins.

Without Ronzo, my life in Morro Bay seemed to have fallen to pieces.

Irene made things worse. She had gone certifiably bonkers since Bernard's death. Or maybe she'd always been bonkers. She was still doing Tarot readings in my store room, but she hadn't done any dire readings for me this week. No swords in my back. I supposed that was a blessing.

She came rushing into the store on Wednesday morning, a little early for her appointment with a Tarot client.

"Something's going on at the *Mary Sue*! There are cops all over the marina. The Coast Guard, too. Maybe they've found out who killed my Bernard. Have you heard anything?"

Since his demise, Bernard had become "hers." So much for denying their affair. I shook my head. Of course I hadn't heard anything more about Bernard's death. Nobody wanted to communicate with me, especially the police.

Gloria, the black-clad owner of the dress shop down the street had come in to grab her special order of the self-help book, *The Road Less Stupid*.

"It's a body. That's why the cops are at the marina." Gloria spoke with a certain amount of relish. "Somebody found a dead body in the dinghy of that yacht that belonged to the dead guy. It was stinking to high heaven."

"Ronzo!" Irene said. "It has to be that gangster boyfriend of yours, Camilla. I told you he killed Boyd Ferrell. I'll bet he's been here all along and killed my Bernard, too. Then somebody whacked him. Probably over those missing diamonds."

"Ronzo? Ronson Zolek?" Gloria looked stricken. "That nice clerk who used to work here before you hired that terrible girl?" Like most customers, Gloria was not enamored of Felicity. I was more than grateful that Felicity didn't work mornings and wasn't there to hear. Plant would get hours of complaints from her about that, and it would all be my fault.

"It couldn't be Mr. Zolek," Gloria said. "This is the body of a Black man. Probably homeless. And nobody whacked him. He died of an overdose or something."

Or something. Like a mass murderer lurking around Morro Bay? I was thinking more strongly about booking that flight to Newark. Maybe I could take Buckingham as an emotional support animal.

"Orion!" Irene jumped in. "It has to be that singer, Orion Jones. Oh, no. Such a good-looking boy!" She managed to sound as if his death was a personal tragedy for her.

Happily, the phone rang, and I could avoid having to comfort Irene over the loss of the man who'd robbed Lupe and torn up my office.

It was Felicity, calling from the café.

"I can't come in this afternoon. I gotta stay here. Lupe's gone bananas. The police came and they want her to look at the body they found on the *Mary Sue*. They're pretty sure it's Orion. So she's all weepy and says she can't come back today if it's him. I can't believe she's so tragified because the guy who ripped her off is dead. Anyway, it's Skip and me all on our lonesomes till seven tonight. It's gonna be cray. And I have to make almond brittle *and* carrot muffins."

"Of course. Lupe needs you more than I do —" I stopped myself. I'd said the dreaded word "need." Plant wouldn't hear the end of it. I felt like telling her to take Thursday off too. And the rest of her life. Because I was going to shut down the store and fly back east.

But I didn't. I knew I didn't have the money. And where would I stay? My New York socialite friends would pretend not to know me. I was stuck here.

Meanwhile, Gloria was staring at me, waving her credit card in my face. The raven-like wings of her elaborate black cape flapped at me.

"Earth to Camilla. What's wrong with you? Are you going to ring up this book or what?"

I couldn't have answered her. I didn't know what was wrong with me. I felt "break-up" like the sailor in the Sloop John B song. I was breaking up like a bad phone signal. And I had no idea how to make sense of my life. I wanted to go home. If I could figure out where the hell that was.

thirty-three

· · ·

A Damn Good Question

The body on the *Mary Sue* was indeed Orion Jones. Dan Fiedler came in on Thursday morning right after I opened the store to tell me about it and buy the latest copy of *Newsweek*. I suppose it was kind of him to bring me the latest news, but he was carrying a take-out cup of coffee from the Otter Café, which I found annoying. I know Barnes and Noble sells coffee in their bookstores, but coffee and books don't actually do well together. I can't sell a book as new if it has coffee stains on it.

"So Orion Jones is definitely dead?" I tried to sound sad. "Lupe's treating it as a personal tragedy, and of course it's terrible when some-body young dies like that, but the man was a criminal. He probably hung around with murderers and one of them got to him. The police can't suspect Ronzo of having anything to do with this one, can they?"

"I have no idea what the Bozos in the Morro Bay P.D. think about anything these days." Dan leaned on my check-out counter. "But I have a friend in the harbor patrol who says they aren't treating it as a homicide. It looks like Orion Jones probably died of an overdose. No visible injuries except post-mortem, probably from seagulls. The body was out there in the dinghy for a few days, he said."

"How did Orion get on board the yacht? I thought the *Mary Sue* was still a crime scene because of Bernard's murder or whatever it was."

"You think a little yellow tape would keep a guy like Orion away?" Dan laughed and took a sip of his coffee.

He always laughed at me. Maybe I was funny. I wouldn't know. Nothing seemed funny to me anymore.

"Why was he on Bernard's boat, anyway?" Probably another stupid question, but I was having trouble making a connection between the elderly White con artist and the up-and-coming young Black musician/thief.

"My friend says it looked as if Orion had been living aboard the yacht for a few days. They found dirty dishes and food he'd brought in from the Marina Café. Plus a lot of beer bottles. Bernard didn't drink beer." Dan looked smug as he imparted this insider knowledge.

"Why do you suppose he'd choose Bernard's boat, though? Had he been there before? Did he even know Bernard?" I still wasn't making sense out of any of this.

Dan looked around the store to make sure it was still empty and spoke in a conspiratorial tone.

"I suspect they had history, those two. Bernard spent some time in the Caribbean, plus they both moved in the New Orleans underground. My client Gene Delacorte says that in the weeks leading up to the theft of his yacht, Bernard had been hanging around with a good-looking young Black guy who fit Orion's description."

This was startling news.

"So maybe Orion was here in Morro Bay to rendezvous with Bernard as much as reconnect with Lupe?"

Dan nodded with increasing animation. He leaned in with both hands on the counter. But I did wish he'd put that coffee cup farther away from the pile of special order books.

"Exactly. Well, the other way around. I think it's more likely Bernard came here to meet up with Orion. He never let on why he'd chosen to come into Morro Bay after his long voyage. He'd intended to sail to San Francisco. I tried to get him to talk about it many times, but he always changed the subject. This is a notoriously difficult harbor to enter, so you really need to want to come here. I think Bernard was in a hurry to unload the diamonds. Probably because he was running out of cash. I've found some evidence that Orion might have had connections with a Chinese jewel smuggling gang in San Francisco. Bernard would have known Orion was going to be here on the Central Coast, because of ads for his winery performances and publicity for his new album."

I had to admit Dan was an impressive detective. What he was saying made sense.

"But the rendezvous went wrong at some point?"

Dan smiled and shrugged as he took another sip of coffee.

I tried to evict Buckingham from my desk chair. I needed to sit down and do some paperwork before the lunchtime rush, but Buckingham wouldn't budge. Maybe he wanted to hear more of Dan's ideas too. These new revelations certainly got my mind working. The possible scenarios were scrolling through my brain like trailers for crime movies.

"So Bernard came into the notorious Morro Bay harbor because he wanted Orion to help him fence the diamonds? What made Bernard change his mind and decide not to give him the diamonds? Maybe Orion wasn't getting him a good enough price from the Chinese people?"

Dan nodded again. "Could be," he said. "But obviously that wasn't okay with Orion. He must have decided to take the diamonds anyway."

"Well, he also decided to take every penny Lupe had in her safe. Do you think he could have been broke?"

Dan took a thoughtful sip of coffee. "I don't know. Maybe he thought the diamonds might be in Lupe's safe, and when they weren't, he took the money instead, like a greedy entitled brat."

I laughed. "Then of course he ransacked my store, plus Skip's place and Raccoon Alice's house, and never found those diamonds. Orion could not have been a happy camper."

Buckingham jumped down from the chair. He didn't seem to approve of my speculations.

But at least Dan seemed to agree. He gave a few more energetic nods.

So I went on. "Do you think Orion was the sailor who took the *Mary Sue* to sea for those five days when it disappeared? You said he was a professional sailor, and he's the only one on our list of suspects."

"Yes," Dan said. "He probably tried to force Bernard to give him the diamonds, then killed him when he didn't get results."

"Then he dumped the body near Pirate's Cove!" I could see the whole scenario now. "He took off the clothing so it would look like Bernard had been indulging in some skinny dipping and drowned accidentally when he swam out too far. Plus of course a nude body couldn't be identified easily."

"That would have been clever." Dan gave me a big smile and bent down to pet Buckingham. "Then Orion brought the *Mary Sue* back here and swam to shore, so it looked as if the yacht had mysteriously reappeared."

"What about the other body at Pirate's Cove? The one Irene thought was Ronzo? How does that fit in?"

Dan shook his head. "I don't think Bernard had anything to do with the hustler's body they found. I don't think Bernard even went to Pirate's Cove before he died."

Wow. Things were falling into place. I wonder if we had the solution to all our mysteries.

"So if Orion killed Bernard, do you think he also killed Boyd Ferrell somehow?" As soon as I said it, I knew it sounded stupid.

"'Somehow?' Like he was wearing an invisibility cloak?" Dan laughed at me again.

Maybe I should be a comedian.

"Well, who do you think killed him?" I closed my desk drawer with businesslike emphasis. "And what if Orion didn't die of an overdose? These can't be three different random killers who decided to murder three men who happened to know each other. Do you really believe Orion overdosed on something when he didn't even seem to be on drugs? Couldn't he have been killed by the same person who killed Boyd?"

Dan looked at me with squinty eyes.

"That's a damn good question," he said. "A damn good question."

"What's a good question?" A woman pushed open the front door and rushed up to the counter. "You mean the question of why you have a bunch of Nazis marching around outside your store?"

Dear Lord. I'd been concentrating on my conversation with Dan and totally failed to notice the crowd of men gathering on the sidewalk outside. They were all dressed in black and had black masks over the lower parts of their faces. They carried signs that said "Freedom Patriots" and "God Hates You" along with some upside-down American flags and a whole bunch of swastikas.

"They must be some more of those anti-vax crazies," Dan said. "Poor Lupe! I'm not sure she can take any more of this. I thought they had finally decided to leave her café alone."

"Oh, they're not picketing the Otter Café," the woman said. "They're picketing this bookstore. The sidewalk in front of the café is clear. I just had a muffin there. They've got these cute carrot muffins with chocolate bats on them for Halloween."

"Halloween! When is Halloween?" I'd totally lost track of the date. I usually wore some sort of costume and had candy for the children who came to the store. With all the drama, I'd forgotten to prepare anything.

"It's tomorrow, dear," the woman said. "Halloween is on Friday this year. The whole town is going to go crazy tomorrow night. I'm staying home."

"Is that why those people outside are all dressed in black?" I petted Buckingham, who had come behind the counter and was looking at me with questioning eyes. He was not any more comfortable with that crowd than I was.

"If those are Halloween costumes," she said with a sniff. "They are in very poor taste." She banged the counter for emphasis and managed to knock over Dan's coffee cup. Luckily it was almost empty, but some spilled on the magazine Dan had bought.

He grabbed the magazine with obvious annoyance as I cleaned up the mess. His jocular mood was gone. "I think you should call the police, Camilla. There are too many of them and they're blocking your sidewalk. I don't understand. Why the hell would Nazis be picketing you?"

"That is a good question." I forced a laugh. "A damned good question."

thirty-four

. . .

The Evil Queen

 I did call the police to say protesters were blocking the sidewalk in front of my store. I knew blocking the sidewalk was against the law because the Morro Bay P.D. cleared a bunch of paparazzi from the walkway a few months before — when my celebrity ex-husband made an unexpected visit. I was much relieved to see my sort-of friend Officer Pilchard arrive an hour later and start clearing the black-clad masked men and their swastika flags from the sidewalk.

He didn't arrest any of them. I guess they weren't breaking any laws except the blocking the sidewalk one. Terrorizing a business owner for no reason didn't seem to be against the law. But he did stay for about an hour outside making sure the "Freedom Patriots" didn't come back to take away the freedom of their fellow citizens to buy books.

I went out and thanked him, but he didn't act like his usual friendly self. I wondered what I'd done to offend him, but I didn't ask. That probably would have offended him. I seemed to offend every-body these days. I was the queen of evil, apparently.

But after that, customers streamed in, maybe out of curiosity. I was grateful Felicity was available to work her regular afternoon shift because I could not have handled all those customers by myself.

Felicity seemed as baffled as I was about the Nazis, but mostly she was worried about Halloween.

"I can't believe you haven't bought any candy yet. You really are losing it. The kids trick-or-treat all up and down Main Street, remember? If we don't have treats, they'll probably TP us or something."

I hadn't thought of that. After the Nazis, the last thing we needed was wet toilet paper strewn all over the front of the store.

I promised her I'd buy plenty of candy and said I'd buy a couple of witch's hats for us. Her expression showed I'd disappointed her again.

"But you don't need to wear it…I mean *have* to wear it." Not 'need,' I told myself. Do not say that word. "Only wear it if it's fun, Felicity. Whatever you want to do is fine…"

It was terrifying trying to talk to her. I had no idea what was going to set off one of her whiny phone calls to Plantagenet telling him how evil I was.

"A witch hat?" Felicity looked down at me with scorn. "That is so lame. We're wearing costumes at the café, and we're all coming as cartoon characters. I have this great Mickey Mouse costume. Lupe is going to be Marge Simpson and Skip is SpongeBob SquarePants. I hope you'll let me wear the Mickey costume here so I don't have to change or anything. There's a costume contest at Fisherman Jack's tomorrow night. So I'll be Mickey Mouse all day. Luckily the costume is pretty comfortable."

"Of course you can wear a Mickey Mouse costume!" I suppose my voice was too enthusiastic, but I was relieved. At least somebody would be in costume for the trick-or-treaters. "What a great idea! I'm so glad Lupe is letting herself have some fun in spite of all this tragedy."

"I don't know if she's having fun. It was Skip's idea, and we made our plans a week ago, before — you know — they found Orion's body."

After I closed the store, and fed Buckingham, I first planned to drive to the supermarket to get some candy, and maybe buy a "lame" witch's hat. But instead, I decided to just walk to the convenience store around the corner. I was so not into the Halloween thing this year. I guess it made me feel alone and miss Ronzo more. Plus I didn't want to play at scary stuff when there might be a real murderer out there, killing people I knew.

Unfortunately, the candy selection at the little shop was pretty depleted, including all the bags of "fun-sized" candy bars. I couldn't afford the full-sized, expensive ones. But the old man behind the counter pointed out a goodly supply of Mexican candy, including *calaveras*, the sugar skulls they made for Day of the Dead. I bought a bunch of little packs of them. And some other colorful candies. I remembered I had a plastic pumpkin left over from last year I could use to display them in the store.

But there were no witch's hats. I was not going to look very festive tomorrow.

On the way home, a strange man in black seemed to be following me. I hoped it wasn't one of the Nazis. Or a homicidal maniac. This was going to be my most terrifying Halloween ever. I was seeing murderers everywhere.

I locked the cottage door and breathed a sigh of relief when I finally got home. Buckingham greeted me with a severe meow. He didn't like me to stray from our routine. We usually ate dinner at the same time.

I microwaved a Lean Cuisine and poured myself a glass of chardonnay. I felt I'd earned it. What a day! What a week. What a month. I was ready for it all to stop.

But of course, as I took my first bite of dry chicken Alfredo, there was a knock on the door. An urgent one. Rap, rap, rap.

I opened the door and there was the evil queen from the *Snow White* movie. An elegant costume, not some plastic Halloween costume from Wal-Mart. And the costumed person wasn't a child.

She stomped right by me into the living room as if she owned the place.

"What the hell is going on, Camilla? You're having a drag queen story time, and you didn't even invite me?"

thirty-five

. . .

Frenemies

It took me a moment to realize the evil queen was Marva — also known as Mistress Nightshade — in heavy make-up and elegant drag. Her voice gave her away. Marva, my friend the drag queen dominatrix. Well, frenemy. I was always a little wary of Marva.

"Get the snifters," she ordered. "I've brought cognac. We need cognac."

I obediently got the Lalique brandy snifters and watched Marva pour a generous amount of Courvoisier in each before sitting on the couch. Buckingham of course, jumped up on her lap. He always preferred men to women. Even when they were in drag.

"But I'm not holding any kind of story time." I took a glass from the coffee table. "What made you think I'm putting on a drag event?"

"You didn't notice your store was picketed by the Freedom Patriots this morning?" She swished the cognac in the snifter before bringing it to her deep red lips. "Their swastikas kind of get people's attention, but I think they hate drag queens even more than they hate Jews or actual trans people. Isn't it amazing how the insurgents who want to overthrow our government call themselves "patriots" and the fascists who want to take away our freedom always put the word "freedom" in their names?"

She was speaking in a kind of hybrid British / snotty-American voice. I guessed that's what evil queens are supposed to sound like. She obviously needed to rant, so I let her go on until she stopped to sip her cognac.

"Of course I saw them," I said. "I had to call the police to get rid of them. Why did they think I was holding a story time event at all? I've never done one. The store is too small, and I don't like having people in my courtyard. Especially after what happened at the Moth thing."

"It was in the newspaper, dear. Well, newsletter — whatever they call it. *The Central Coast Wire.* I'm not sure they actually print it on paper, but you can find it online. She pulled her phone from her tote bag, which I now noticed was shaped like a big, red apple, to go with her costume.

"Here," she said after tapping the phone a few times. "Here's the story. It came out yesterday. They said they were contacted by the owner of the store. As far as I know, you're the only owner of the Morro Bay Bookshop."

She handed me her phone, and there was an article with the headline, "Morro Bay Bookshop to Hold Drag Storybook Hour."

"You can see why I felt a little hurt." Marva sniffed, dropping her queenly persona. "After all, we're supposed to be friends, and you didn't even ask me to help."

Marva's dominatrix personality was usually so strong, I was surprised to see her acting vulnerable. I had the sudden realization she might be the only person I could trust right now.

"Of course we're friends." I leaned over and grabbed her hand. "And I need one right now. A sane one. I really need somebody to talk to."

Sane. I'd just told a drag queen who spanked men for a living that she was my sanest friend.

"Is Plantagenet down in LA again?"

I shook my head and took a sip of my cognac. It would be better if he simply were out of town. And I didn't feel like I was going bonkers.

"No. He and Silas are home in San Luis. But my new employee, Felicity, keeps phoning them and whining about what a bad boss I am. At length. So he's mad at both of us. And I keep misplacing things.

And I totally forgot tomorrow is Halloween. I couldn't even find a witch's hat."

"You forgot about getting a Halloween costume? Is that all? Oh, sweetie, I have just the thing. I happen to have an extra costume in my car. I was going to wear it for one of my clients, but he cancelled. Shall I get it?"

Oh, dear. I hoped it wasn't going to be one of her "powerful women" costumes she specialized in, like Hillary Clinton and Margaret Thatcher. I didn't want to get into any political discussions with my customers. But I was grateful she had something to lend me.

She came back in a few minutes carrying a long garment bag and a pair of black leather boots. The boots looked big, but maybe I could stuff the toes. With a flourish, she pulled off the garment bag and showed me what looked like a pirate costume. With a long, curly black wig, a three-cornered hat, and a hook with a handle inside. I did not want to know what she'd intended to do with that.

"You can be Captain Hook!" She plopped the hat on my head. "You'll be adorable. There's a mustache in there along with the wig. Or you can draw one on with eye pencil if it's too uncomfortable."

We went back to my bedroom where I scrambled into the costume, and it fit amazingly well. The boots felt like clown shoes, but if I stuffed some socks in there, I could probably keep them on for most of the day. I wasn't sure about the wig. It felt scratchy. And I was not going to paste a mustache on my face or I wouldn't be able to drink or eat all day. But the coat, pants, and hat were perfect.

"Avast, ye maties!" I raised my cognac in a salute to Marva.

"Oh, you look fabulous in drag!" Marva laughed and reached into her bag and brought out an eye pencil. "Let me give you a cute little mustache." She proceeded to draw on my face.

"Am I in drag? Yes, I guess I am cross-dressing here. Drag is just a costume, isn't it?"

"Duh." Marva finished and admired her handiwork. "Lose the wig," she said. "Your own hair is the right length. Nobody said pirates can't be blonde."

That's when we heard the commotion outside in the courtyard. Men's voices. Then the sound of breaking glass.

Buckingham came running in from the front room and dove under my bed.

I ran and peeked out the front window. The man in black who had been following me earlier was there, ushering ten or twelve men from the driveway into the courtyard. The swastikas started to unfurl.

A feeling of utter hopelessness froze me where I stood. They'd only broken one of the floodlights I had aimed at the patio, but why? Why did I have to put up with evil, stupid people who had nothing better to do than make my life hell?

I felt Marva's hand on my shoulder — warm and reassuring.

"Looks like your Nazis are back. I'll handle them. You call 911." Her voice took on a deep, masculine tone as she reached into her poison apple tote bag and pulled out what looked like an army issue SIG Sauer pistol. Sometimes I'd forget that Marva — or rather Marvin — and Ronzo had served together in Afghanistan.

"These Bozos turn into little 'fraidy cats when they meet a real soldier." Now back to being Marvin, he pulled off his crown and wimple and stomped out into the hallway with a macho swagger. No more drag queen. He looked like a he-man dressed in a silly costume for Halloween.

He opened the front door and shouted, "Hey a**holes, you're trespassing. The cops are on their way." I heard the sound of a gunshot. Good Lord. Please let that gun be Marvin's.

I ducked behind the couch, just in case, and punched 911 into my phone, feeling deeply grateful that I had a frenemy like Marvin.

thirty-six

. . .

Wackadoodles

After the police evicted the last few swastika waving "patriots" from my courtyard, Marva came back to my living room, settled into the couch, and filled our snifters with another generous pour of Courvoisier.

"Thank goodness the wackadoodles are gone," she said. "They might not be afraid of the police, but I think I put some fear into them, thanks to my little friend here." She pointed to the gun, which she'd put on the coffee table next to the cognac.

I was not happy she'd fired it, but I'm sure she hadn't aimed at anybody. If that's what it took to be wackadoodle-free, so be it. Here we were, talking about crazy people: Captain Hook and Snow White's evil stepmother. If somebody walked in, they'd think we were the wacky ones.

I took a deep breath. "I don't know what I would have done if you hadn't been here, Marva. Or what they might have done. I so much didn't need those horrible people to come right to my home after the kind of week I've had." I took a generous swallow of cognac.

"Well, I'm glad I could solve your problems with a pirate costume and a warning shot from my trusty pistol." She was back to her Marva voice. "Earlier I thought maybe you were suffering from depression because of all these dead bodies that keep piling up around here. That guy they found yesterday — Orion Jones — he sang in the café right down the street, didn't he? You must have known him. Was he a friend? He certainly was dishy."

"Oh yes. I knew Orion. In fact, according to Lupe next door, I was having an affair with him."

Marva arched an eyebrow. "Really? Were you cheating on my friend Ronson?"

"No. No. Of course not. I would never cheat on Ronzo. Besides, Orion was barely in his twenties. And of course I'm worried about all the deaths. Plus the fact some homicidal maniac is out there and the police won't catch him because they are so sure Ronzo is the culprit."

"Yeah. Where the hell is Zolek?" Marva looked around the room, as if she expected Ronzo to materialize from somewhere. She motioned to Buckingham, who was peeking into the living room, checking to see if the coast was clear. "Why isn't Ronzo telling the police they're dead wrong? And protecting your reputation? He's always been so reliable. Does he need a good lawyer?"

Buckingham jumped up on her lap and started to purr. Maybe he was soothed by the sound of Ronzo's name.

I sighed and gave Marva a slightly weepy account of what happened after Boyd's murder and how Ronzo disappeared into the New Jersey underground when he was named a person of interest by Morro Bay's finest.

"So he's not even on this coast, and they still think he's killing all these people in California? Doesn't anybody in the Morro Bay P.D. have a brain?"

I gave a defeated laugh. "I guess he's supposed to teleport back and forth from New Jersey or something. I don't know. I don't know anything, except that I'm going bonkers, and I never contacted the *Central Coast Wire* with news about a story time event. I didn't even know that newspaper existed."

"I wish nobody did. I only go to their website to see what horrors they're up to now." Marva picked up her glass. "These people are such cowards. They hide behind fake names and cover their faces with those stupid masks. They won't wear masks to keep from spreading a plague but they'll do it to march around and say 'heil Hitler' to drag queens."

"So these people are anti-vax, too? Do you think that's why they picked my store? The paper must have made up the story that I called them. It's an absurd lie. Maybe they chose me because I'm almost next door to Lupe and the police have been keeping the anti-vaxxers away from her café since they set her on fire."

"They set her on fire?" Marva's well-defined eyebrows rose. "Oh, yes. I guess I heard about that. I wasn't sure I could believe it. They really did that? How awful. Wackadoodles seem to be everywhere these days. Lupe has been through a lot recently, hasn't she?"

"Yes. I guess I should be more empathetic. Maybe that's why she went so completely bonkers and accused me of sleeping with her godson." I tried to be kind, but even talking about Lupe these days put me on edge. I was always afraid she'd show up at my door and scream at me some more. It's so terrifying to be hated for something you didn't do.

Marva sipped cognac and gave me a contemplative look.

"I need to hear more about what's happening with Ronzo," she said. "This isn't making much sense to me. He went to New Jersey for a new job with this man Cassius Burgh, found out he's suspected of murder out here, so he went to stay with some mobbed-up cousins. And now he hasn't communicated with you for — what? A month?"

"Not a word. I guess he's afraid the police will track my phone calls and find him."

"But somehow this private eye Fiedler has managed to talk to him?"

"I guess Ronzo was able to communicate with him, since the police wouldn't be monitoring Dan Fiedler's phone. After all, they have no reason to think the two men have a connection."

"Ah." Marva swished the last bit of cognac in the glass, then finished it. "I suppose that makes sense, but why hasn't he given Fiedler messages for you? And what happened to Cassius Burgh?"

I hadn't thought about why Ronzo didn't give Dan a message for me. "I think Dan Fiedler only talked to Ronzo that one time, when he was in New Jersey. As far as Mr. Burgh, I don't have a clue. Nobody's talking about him, so I guess he's not a 'person of interest' anymore."

"I don't think you should trust that guy Fiedler. He's been nosing around some of my clients' yachts down at the Marina. Gives off a creepy vibe."

Marva set down her glass. "And stay away from Lupe. I don't trust her either. Some days at the café she's all sweetness and light and other days…the Wicked Witch of the West. I think one of those two might have fed the drag story time lie to that fascist rag, knowing the Freedom Patriots would picket you. The *Wire's* news is pretty iffy — mostly Kremlin propaganda — but I don't think they usually make up stories out of nothing. Something had to have sparked the article. I think they really got an email about a drag event at your bookstore from somebody."

That was a disconcerting thought.

"Okay, but why? Why would Lupe or Dan hate me that much?"

"If Lupe thinks you secretly boinked her godson, there's your motive right there: revenge. If Fiedler did it…I don't know. I haven't figured that guy out yet."

Dear Lord. She was right. Of course. Somebody planted that story. On purpose. Pretending to be me. Somebody who had a grudge against me. I wondered if they were responsible for those dreadful Amazon "reviews," too. And all the other things that made me feel I was losing my mind.

Lupe was my number one suspect in Boyd's murder. Now I wondered if she was responsible for all the crazy-making things that had been happening to me. And what if it wasn't an overdose, and she'd killed Orion for stealing her money, and Bernard, too? Maybe Lupe Sorensen was a serial killer.

Unless the killer was the enigmatic Dan Fiedler.

And what really happened to Cassius Burgh?

thirty-seven

. . .

Happy Halloween

My Captain Hook costume was a success. Customers loved it. They also seemed to like the novelty of my Mexican candies. And much to my astonishment, even Felicity seemed to approve. She was kind of adorable in her Mickey Mouse costume.

Not that customers were buying many books, but that was okay. It was all good publicity, after the weird stuff that happened with the Freedom Patriots. They seemed to be gone — for now. But the results of that bizarre article in the *Central Coast Wire* were still with me.

"When is your drag story time going to happen? Is it today?" A woman dressed as Wednesday Addams leaned on the counter. "I have two nephews who would love to come. Are you going to do the reading?"

"Her?" Felicity gave a derisive laugh. "She not a drag queen. She's an actual woman."

"But she's dressed as a man." Wednesday turned and gave Felicity the once over. "And so are you. Mickey Mouse and Captain Hook are both male."

"That's right." I laughed and spoke in a way too cheerful voice. "We're drag kings."

Felicity snorted. "That's silly. There's no such thing." She turned away and went to the back table to rearrange the remaindered books.

"That's because she's a mouse, not a man," I said *sotto voce* to Wednesday. A funny joke, I thought. But I hoped Felicity hadn't heard me, or Plant would get endless whining about it. Well, at least I was actually guilty of insulting her this time. I guess being dressed as a pirate made me forget my manners.

"You're both disgusting, is what I say." An older man stomped toward the counter. "You people are corrupting children. Grooming them to become gay."

"I have to agree with him," another woman said. "Drag events for children are revolting. Why do you have to shove your lifestyle down their little throats?"

"My lifestyle? You think I'm gay because I'm dressed as a pirate for Halloween?"

Wednesday shook her head and took off without buying anything.

"You're having those drag story time events. That's because you want to convert children to your way of life." The old man pounded the counter to emphasize his belief in his delusions.

"That's right! If children spend any time around her, they'll become etiquette experts who run bookstores!" This comment came from a rather pretty woman in a 1950s suit and matching hat. With a suspiciously deep voice. She turned to the man at the counter. "I used to work here. Can I help you find a book today sir?"

It was Plantagenet, being his old wonderful self. His question was a great way to remind the deluded man that a bookstore is a place to buy books, not get free candy and harass the staff. I watched Plant lead the man to the Westerns section and deposit him there.

Plant came back to the counter and offered me a gloved hand. Doeskin. My mother had a pair of gloves like that.

"Lois," he said. "Lois Lane. Clark Kent is browsing in the cookbook section."

I looked over and saw Silas in a double-breasted suit, wearing a pair of dark-framed glasses and a fedora with a tag stuck in the band that said, "Press."

"We're on our way to a Halloween party in Cambria and I thought

I'd stop in and make sure you're all right. I heard about your visit from the Nazis. Are you really hosting a drag story time? I'm surprised you'd have another event here after the last one ended so unfortunately."

"No. Of course we're not having a drag story event. Where would I put all those people?" I said this way too loud, hoping the bigots would hear. I turned back to Plant. "We don't have that big a children's book section anyway. I'd like to have more of a selection, but most of our customers are older people looking for beach reads. I typically only sell children's books to grandparents to give the grandkids at Christmas.

"Why do people think you're having this story time thing? It was all over the news last night."

"Somebody sent in a story to a local newspaper called the *Central Coast Wire*. Nobody knows who. Somebody who doesn't like me, obviously. Maybe the same person who set the anti-vaxxers on Lupe a few weeks ago."

I could see the concern in Plant's face through the Lois Lane make-up.

"Something really doesn't add up, Camilla. A guy was murdered here — what? Six weeks ago? Then your regular customer ends up mysteriously dead at Pirate's Cove, and the singer at the café next door tries to rob you and ends up dead. And there are all these bizarre protests going on here and at the café. It can't only be bad luck. Somebody's got to be orchestrating this."

"Lupe. I think it's Lupe Sorensen." Marva, in her wicked queen drag, had materialized behind Plant. "I was just talking to her at the café. She makes a fabulous Marge Simpson. With that blue beehive wig, she has to be seven feet tall. But she's bananas. Completely wacko. She's sure you seduced Orion, and thinks you're hiding those diamonds. Deluded people are dangerous. She knows how bad it is for business to have a bunch of protesters outside — from recent experience. She probably figured planting that story was an easy way to get revenge. She practically confessed it to me."

"Oh, dear. You could be right. She'd know being picketed is bad for business, all right. And it's kind of terrifying."

"Kind of? It's scary as hell." Plant made a grim face. "Nobody should play games with Nazis. They're capable of anything. I think you should ask the police to keep an officer here. Harassment is against the law. Halloween is supposed to be scary, but not like that."

I felt a chill. I really was afraid. Those lunatics could come back at any time. Whoever was harassing me was doing a good job of it.

thirty-eight

. . .

The Medusa Smile

As a rule, I am a non-confrontational person, but I also don't believe in letting feelings fester. I wasn't sure if Lupe had planted the false drag story time lies in the *Wire*, but I knew that hiding from her wasn't going to help.

On Monday morning after Halloween, I went to the Otter Café before I opened my store and ordered a latte and a muffin. I knew Lupe would be on her own, because she gave Felicity Mondays off.

Lupe was dressed in uncharacteristic black, and looked as if she was continuing the Halloween celebrations by dressing as Elvira, Mistress of the Dark.

Her demeanor was icy as she prepared my coffee. It wasn't since my debutante days that I'd known anybody who could freeze you to your bones with a smile.

It was a few moments before I could move or speak. I finally thought of something polite to say as I paid for my coffee and muffin with cash, a gesture that all merchants appreciate in these days of big credit card swipe fees.

"Halloween seemed to have been a big success on this block." I gave her my best Manners Doctor smile. "I think it was great fun that your staff all dressed as cartoon characters."

Lupe paused a moment and narrowed her eyes. "That was Skip's idea. I didn't want to go ahead with it, since I'm in mourning for my godson. I can't believe you're going ahead with your life as if nothing happened, when your lover has just died. What color is that you're wearing — hot pink?"

I was wearing a rose-colored cashmere sweater set with gray slacks, so I didn't reply, except to thank her for the muffin. I started for a vacant table by the window, but she came out from behind the counter and stopped me.

"That's a to-go cup I gave you. So go." She shot eye daggers at me.

"I never exchanged more than a few words with your godson," I said in as polite tone as I could muster. "He was certainly not my lover. But of course it's tragic how he died. I'm very sorry for your loss. He was a wonderful singer."

I walked as fast as I could without actually running and made it to the courtyard behind my store, where Buckingham was waiting for me. I had to put the coffee and muffin on the back step so I could unlock the door. Buckingham sniffed them and backed off as if he'd smelled something awful.

That did not bode well.

I took the muffin and coffee to my office and put them on the desk. But now I didn't want to touch them. Could she have poisoned them? Her attitude had certainly been poisonous. In an overabundance of caution, I tossed the muffin in the bin, poured the coffee down the bathroom sink, and fired up the old Mr. Coffee for my regular cup of perfectly acceptable brew. I had a protein bar in the desk drawer I could eat later if I got hungry.

At this point, I was pretty sure Lupe was a murderer. So it was perfectly logical she'd try to kill me too. I was pretty sure she'd lured Boyd Ferrell to Morro Bay because she hated him for what he did to Verline. From what Felicity told me, Lupe's story of wanting to rekindle an old romance was pure fiction. I didn't know what Lupe's motive for killing Bernard would have been, but if she was capable of one murder, she was capable of two. Especially if there were diamonds involved. Maybe she killed Bernard while trying to get the diamonds Orion was supposed to fence. And Orion? She was acting so "tragified" about his death, as Felicity put it, but the man had lied to her, burglarized her café, and betrayed her. Perhaps the lady did mourn too much?

That was it. The truth was, I lived next door to a murderer and nobody was safe. Plant was probably right. I needed to talk to the police about what I knew, even though it was unlikely they'd believe me.

But first I had a store to open.

And who should come sauntering in as soon as I unlocked the front door at ten AM, but Dan Fiedler. I tried to act pleased to see him, but I was not prepared to play his brand of conversational combat.

"So, do you know why you had that visit from the Third Reich on Thursday?" He gave me a big grin as if the incident had been in some way amusing. "You do seem to collect a lot of enemies."

He held out a paper bag from the Otter Café that was full of almond brittle.

"Have some? It's great for anger management."

I hesitated a moment, then took a piece. Lupe wouldn't have poisoned a whole batch of almond brittle on the off chance I'd be given a piece. After I'd done some crunching, I gave him a serious look.

"I do have enemies. And I think I know who they are. Or rather she is."

"She? Who do you think it is?"

I knew nobody else was in the store, but I still felt the need to whisper.

"I think it's Lupe. Somebody contacted a newspaper called the *Central Coast Wire* and told them I was holding a drag queen storybook thing. It's a rabid right-wing newsletter and whoever planted that story would have known the news would reach the Neo-Nazis. She still thinks I had a hot and heavy thing going with Orion, and this morning she nearly knifed me when I went into the café for coffee and a muffin.

"Are you all right?" Dan's eyebrows went up. "She knifed you?"

"Not for real. But I suspect she might have tried to poison me. I threw the coffee and muffin away."

"But you're eating her almond brittle."

I'd already taken another piece from his bag.

"She might poison me, but she wouldn't have any reason to poison you. Unless you had an imaginary rendezvous with Orion, too."

Dan smiled. "Not a major possibility. Even for her active imagination. I guess you're safe." He held out the bag to offer more. "Besides, Felicity makes all the almond brittle. Lupe usually bakes the muffins, but Felicity has been doing the almond brittle for months. It's her recipe."

How strange that Felicity hadn't crowed about that particular talent. Usually, she was good at tooting her own horn.

"Anyway, I figure Lupe knew how awful it was to get picketed by fanatics, since it happened to her, too. I think she lost a lot of business to those anti-vaxxers." She'd never talked about how much business they drove away, but I figured it had to be a lot. They drove away my customers too.

"I don't think it bothered her that much. I happen to think she called the anti-vaxxers on herself." Dan looked annoyingly smug.

"Why would she do that? They even set her dress on fire."

"It sure drew attention away from her relationship with Boyd Ferrell, didn't it?"

"Drew attention away? You mean…" I stopped for a moment, wondering if he was saying what I thought he was saying. "You think Lupe killed Boyd Ferrell?"

Dan gave me a lopsided smile.

"It had crossed my mind."

This was interesting. "Then it looks like she could be a serial killer. Doesn't it?"

"I don't know about that, but I think she has Gene's diamonds somewhere…" Dan stopped himself when Gloria wafted into the store looking for a book on decluttering. She wasn't wearing black today, but autumnal colors of beige and brown. She looked more like a sparrow than a raven.

"I do hope all that nonsense from the protesters is over," she said. "Maybe it will be getting too chilly for them this month. I guess even lunatics need to get out of the house and get some exercise once in a while. But I'm awfully tired of our neighborhood getting picketed for no good reason."

"We all are," Dan said. "Would you like some almond brittle?" He held out the bag to her.

She looked at him as if he were offering her a bag of seagull guano and shook her head.

"I don't go to the Otter Café anymore. I can't abide any of them. Well, except for that nice boy Skip. But they all act like it's such a hardship to deal with customers. They don't know how to smile and say 'have a nice day.' I was trained at Macy's, you know. In Palo Alto. We were taught to count out change, in case the electric went out, and we always said 'have a nice day.' People appreciate the little things."

"Yes, they do." I gave her a big smile. "Now let me help you find that book. Are you looking for something by Marie Kondo?"

After Gloria left with a copy of *Spark Joy*, Dan still hovered around the counter.

"If you think Lupe poisoned your latte and muffin, I could get them analyzed. Would you like me to do that?"

This was an odd offer. It had to cost a private detective a lot for a laboratory analysis.

"I don't have the coffee, but I have the cup and the muffin in the bin in my office. But I'm not sure they were really poisoned. She didn't have much time, and she'd have to be good at sleight-of-hand. But she gave me such a poisonous smile."

"I know that smile," he said. "It completely freezes you."

"The Medusa smile," I said. "I know exactly what you mean."

thirty-nine

. . .

Beach Rocks

I'd asked Marva to stop by to pick up the Captain Hook costume around 7:30 on Wednesday evening, after I'd had it dry-cleaned. I assumed she was early when there was a knock on the door at 7:00, just as I was eating my re-heated chicken parmesan.

But the person at the door wasn't Marva, but Irene, with Raccoon Alice in tow. Alice's eye make-up looked Halloween-y in the glow from my porch light.

"Alice wants those samples back," Irene announced. "We think your store is attracting bad energy, and nothing in the area is safe."

"I'm criticized by Nazis, so that means I'm a bad person?" I spoke without thinking. A mistake. I really didn't want to argue with those two. "Sorry. It's a touchy subject. It's upsetting when people make up lies about you. But of course. I'll get you the crystals and cards. They do belong to you, Alice. And I have no idea when or if Ronzo will be back to choose some New Age inventory."

Buckingham slipped out as I held the door. I hoped he'd stay safely in the courtyard. He wasn't supposed to go out at night.

"I've kept your things in the safe in my office," I told Alice. "I'm so sorry Ronzo hasn't been back. I'm worried about him and miss him terribly."

Irene gave a snort and Alice said nothing as I led them through the courtyard to the back of the store. I unlocked the door and ushered them into my office. Alice's things were easy to spot in the back. They were still in the ancient gift bag Alice had brought them in. The bag looked as if it was going to fall apart at the seams, and the sparkling red and green elves were suffering from serious glitter mange.

I suppose I shouldn't have been surprised when the bottom tore out of the bag as I pulled it out of the safe. Maybe the ladies were right about the store's "bad energy." Luckily most of the crystals were in their own box, with separate compartments, and labels indicating their powers. The four boxes of Tarot cards slid along the linoleum toward the desk, but the cards only escaped from one. Alice bent down and picked up two intact boxes and put them in her purse.

"These old decks can be valuable, you know." Alice gave a harrumph.

"Yes. You told us. That's why I've been keeping them in the safe."

I put the box of crystals on the desk and retrieved the other Tarot cards. There was also the small cardboard box with the bigger crystals inside. It sat on the remnants of the Christmas bag on the floor.

Alice gathered the other Tarot cards and put them in her pockets, while Irene clutched the box of crystals to her bosom.

"Thank goodness these are all safe and sound." Irene gave a weary sigh.

"What about these?" Still kneeling on the floor, I held up the small box.

Hands full, Irene shook her head. "Don't worry about those. You can have them. Just some rocks Bernard picked up on the beach. They had sentimental value for him, I guess. He wanted me to keep them safe, but honestly, I can't imagine why. They don't have any value to me, and he's gone, so you can have them. Maybe you can sell them to the tourists along with abalone shells and some nice sea glass jewelry. Those would go over well with tourists."

No. I wasn't going to sell sea glass and shells. Plenty of other shops took care of that sort of thing, but I thanked her for the suggestion. I locked the safe and took the box back to my cottage as I said as polite a farewell to the ladies as I could muster. Their primitive superstitions were unpleasant, and Irene's assumption that she knew more about business than I did was annoying. So was the implication that I was somehow responsible for all these unfortunate events.

As I sat down to my now-cold dinner, there was another knock on the door.

This time it really was Marva, right on time. But she showed up at my door in an unexpected costume: khakis, a blazer and a buzz cut. This was Marvin, looking like an ordinary forty-five-year-old man. He had a purring Buckingham in his arms. I let them both inside.

Marvin's unmade-up face showed emotion better than usual. I could see intense worry in his eyes.

"I've been trying to get hold of Ronzo, and I've got bad news." He pushed through and plunked himself down at my dining table. "You got any wine?"

I pulled a bottle of *pinot grigio* out of the fridge and put two glasses on the table, as if we were celebrating something, but I didn't feel good about any of this.

"What's happened? Is he in jail or something?"

"Or something," Marvin said. "It seems like the Croatians who were hiding him don't want him to leave."

"What? Is that why he's been incommunicado for so long?" My body felt cold all over. Was Ronzo a prisoner?

"Looks like it. I know some vets in his area and I asked about the people he's been staying with. They sound like low-life scum. Trafficking is one of their main sources of income, and they are not always loyal to their own. If they help somebody from the old country, they can force them into virtual slavery. My friends say it may have happened to Ronzo because he speaks some Croatian. Plus he's a computer guy and he's good at finding people."

Slavery. Trafficking. Ronzo was a prisoner. This was too horrible to get my brain around.

I looked at the cold chicken on my plate, surrounded by congealed sauce and limp spinach, and felt sick to my stomach.

"I — oh, no. I wasn't prepared for this. I guess. I do attract bad energy, don't I?" I picked up the glass of wine Marvin had pushed toward me. "What am I going to do? It's not like the police can rescue him, is it?"

"Not likely," Marvin said, "But maybe I can. I've got a ticket to fly to Newark tonight. Would you be able to drive me to the airport in fifteen, twenty minutes? Parking there costs an arm and a leg."

Tonight. Marvin wasn't one to waste time whining. He meant business.

"Of course." I took away my sad plate and scraped the contents into the garbage.

Marvin sauntered into the living room, sipping his wine, as if what he'd told me hadn't shattered my world. He picked up the brown card-board box.

"I have a box like this." He laughed. "It has all the nuts and bolts and Allen wrenches left over from putting together Ikea furniture." He opened the box and picked up one of the rocks.

"Those are some beach rocks that belonged to Bernard that Irene and Alice didn't want —" I stopped as I watched Marvin in horror. He'd apparently become afflicted with sudden case of St. Vitus Dance. He stamped his feet and made a whistling noise and appeared to be losing his balance. He took another rock out of the box and held it up to my reading lamp.

"Oh, Camilla, sweetie, do you have any idea what you've got here?"

"Some kind of beach rocks. Irene says Bernard picked them up at Moonstone Beach."

"Did he now?" Marvin laughed. "I'd love to know what part of that beach produces three of the hugest uncut diamonds I've ever seen."

"Diamonds? Those things are diamonds?"

"About a billion dollars' worth, honey. Probably a billion and a half. Let's put them in your nice little safe before we go to the airport, okay?"

forty

. . .

A Person of Interest

I had trouble getting to sleep after Marvin's revelations. Was Ronzo really imprisoned by dangerous gangsters — enslaved and unable to communicate? Maybe Marvin had been overly dramatizing the situation, but if Ronzo was a prisoner, I was terrified for him.

Then there was Marvin's other little revelation that I had a billion dollars' worth of diamonds in my safe. That terrified me too. I had to phone Dan Fiedler in the morning and tell him I'd had the diamonds all along. I wanted them off my property ASAP. They could have been the source of the "bad energy" Irene and Alice said was attracting unpleasantness to the store. Thrillers were full of stories of dangerous jewels that caused havoc to anybody who owned them.

Okay, I didn't know if I believed in rocks sending out bad juju, but I knew I wanted those things gone. They would attract thieves. Like poor Orion. And then I had to think of Mr. Delacorte, who lost his wife and his yacht in all this, and deserved to have his diamonds back.

I tossed and turned so much, Buckingham escaped to the living room to sleep on the couch. When I got up in the morning, bleary-eyed from lack of sleep, he was curled up on a throw pillow, and gave me a disapproving meow.

After two cups of coffee and an English muffin, I made my way over to the store. I was almost afraid to go into my office, as if the diamonds were Kryptonite that would radiate that bad juju right into my soul.

I phoned Dan, but only got voicemail. I was afraid to use the word "diamonds" for fear of somebody listening in. I didn't know who. Croatian gangsters maybe. Perhaps they'd tapped my phone. I had no idea what they knew about me, if anything. So I simply told Dan I had some news for him.

It was afternoon before he arrived, and Felicity was working, busily tidying up things that didn't need tidying. I told her Dan and I had business in the office and she gave me a dramatic eye-roll that looked as if it hurt her head, but I ignored it. She was always implying that I was interested in men other than Ronzo. Maybe projecting her own sexual neediness.

Dan was eager to talk. "Have you heard from Ronzo? What's your news?" He looked genuinely worried, which didn't help with my anxiety about those gangsters.

But I gave him a big smile and opened the safe with a dramatic flourish. "Some stories have happy endings," I announced. I brought out the brown cardboard box and presented it to him. "Happy Birthday to you. Or to Mr. Delacorte, I guess."

Dan opened the box and gave an appropriate gasp.

"How did you find them? What did you do? Did you get them from Lupe?"

I had to tell him they'd been in my safe the whole time with Alice's woo-woo samples and I didn't recognize them as diamonds until a visiting friend set me straight.

"Alice gave you these and doesn't have a clue what they are? How did she get them?"

"They're sort of Irene's, I think. She said Bernard picked them up on Moonstone Beach and they had sentimental value, so he asked her to take care of them."

Dan laughed. "That Bernard really was a cagey Cajun. That's what Gene Delacorte called him. Bernard probably figured those ladies would refuse to take care of billions worth of diamonds, but worthless rocks with sentimental value —

they'd take super good care of them."

That made sense. I would have thought the same way. I'm so glad I hadn't known something so valuable had been stored in my safe. I would have been wild with anxiety. But I'd happily take special care of something worthless that had sentimental value to a friend.

Dan kept staring at the diamonds in their utilitarian box.

"You know, I'm glad to know Lupe didn't steal them. I think we've been maligning that woman for no good reason. This morning, I found out she has an alibi for Orion's demise. I finally got a time of death from a friend at the coroner's office. It was between eight AM and noon on the Friday before they found the body. And Lupe was at the café all day. I was at the café having breakfast that morning around nine, and Felicity had the morning off, so Lupe was running ragged. She ran out of almond brittle and was trying to make it herself, but she couldn't find the candy thermometer. She looked totally overwhelmed. I can't imagine how she would be able to sneak off and murder anybody. Especially somebody on a boat moored in the harbor."

"Are they finally saying it's a murder? I thought they were claiming it was an overdose."

"I think so. They haven't done an autopsy yet, but what they first thought was a post-mortem wound from a bird turned out to be a stab wound, and he lost a lot of blood. So it wasn't an overdose, accidental or otherwise."

"You don't think Lupe could have sneaked off for an hour and stabbed him the way she killed Boyd?"

"She sneaked out, stole a dinghy, rowed out to the *Mary Sue*, stabbed Orion and went back to baking muffins?" Dan gave a grim smile. "I don't think so. And I have to say I never saw her near Boyd after the story-telling on the Moth night. She was too busy restocking the refreshments."

"Then we're kind of running out of suspects, aren't we?" I was beginning to despair. Things were pointing back to Ronzo looking like Boyd's killer again. "You can't suspect Skip or Felicity or the other café staff?"

He gave a small laugh. "No, but I do suspect Cassius Burgh. That's the man who had the strongest motive to kill Boyd. Burgh had been in love with Verline. She left New Jersey soon after Boyd's attack, and as far as I know, Burgh never saw her again. And what he didn't know until recently was that she had been pregnant with his child when she got that horrific beating."

"She lost a baby as well as her health and her career? How awful." I had to admit I was just as happy Boyd was dead. He sounded like a truly horrible person.

Dan shook his head. "No. Somehow the baby survived. The baby was Orion Jones."

I hesitated a minute to take this in. "Orion's father was Cassius Burgh?"

"Or so Mr. Burgh believes. That's how Orion got the recording contract with Pacific Records. Singer-songwriters and folk musicians aren't their thing. Their artists mostly do hip-hop and rap. But apparently Orion showed up at Burgh's office about seven months ago and announced he was Burgh's son and bulldozed his way into a contract. Other people at Pacific Records weren't pleased.

"Oh, wow. You've been doing a lot of sleuthing, haven't you?" I had to sit down. This had some nasty implications. If Burgh had killed Boyd, and Orion had definitely been murdered — were they related? "Could Cassius Burgh have somehow come back to Morro Bay without anybody knowing — and killed his own son? Why would he do that?"

Dan shrugged. "Maybe he'd found out Orion wasn't his son after all."

"There's no DNA proof or anything?"

"Not that the people at Pacific Records know about. They have been highly skeptical of Orion this whole time."

This was all getting really creepy. "Do you suppose Cassius Burgh is still in Morro Bay? I wonder if the Morro Bay police still consider him a person of interest along with Ronzo."

"He'd certainly be a person of interest to me." Dan gave a smug smile. "But luckily none of it has anything to do with me. Thanks to you, I have the diamonds. No more tedious detective work. Now I get to give the good news to Mr. Delacorte."

And I needed to find a way to get the police to see that Mr. Burgh, and not Ronzo, was probably guilty of Boyd Ferrell's murder. I had no idea how I was going to do that, but it needed to be done.

forty-one

. . .

Get-Away

"You gave Dan Fiedler two billion dollars' worth of diamonds? Without even checking to find out if he really was working for the owner? Camilla, you really do have Wonder Bread for brains." Felicity was giving me one of her epic eye-rolls.

"Just a billion and a half, according to my friend Marva." Wonder Bread for brains. I hadn't heard that particular insult since my debutante years.

"Marva. A drag queen. You get your financial advice from a drag queen?" Felicity shook her head and went back to attacking imaginary dust bunnies under the remainder table.

I obviously should not have told her about the diamonds. I thought she might be relieved that particular chapter of our lives was over. And, well, she asked what Dan and I had been doing in my office all that time, so I wanted to tell her what really happened.

But it had never occurred to me that Dan might not be working for Delacorte. Or to question whether Delacorte existed. I do not have a particularly suspicious mind. But Felicity did. I guess growing up on the streets would do that to you. In the old days I would have talked it over with Plantagenet before parting with the diamonds. But without him as a sounding board, it was as if I couldn't hear my own voice. Or make my own decisions.

I spent the rest of the afternoon in the office, avoiding Felicity. Maybe she was right, and something was wrong with me. I was sleep-walking through my own life. I didn't trust myself to do anything right these days. I almost believed Felicity when she insisted the Manners Doctor was an elderly lady living in New York, and I only imagined writing all those columns and books.

I left the door to my office open, so I could hear what was going on in the store. But there wasn't much traffic — until about four-thirty, when I heard something of a commotion out there. Then silence.

A few minutes later, I heard Plantagenet's voice saying, "Knock, knock! Can I come in, darling? I hear you just gave away a billion and a half dollars' worth of diamonds. I can't believe you had a billion and a half dollars' worth of diamonds and didn't give me any."

I stood to hug Plant and something about his strong arms and familiar scent made me start to cry like an infant. I just blubbered.

"It's all right, darling," He stroked my messy hair. "I can see some-thing's going on with you. You're going to need some help. Maybe some good drugs. Silas takes an antidepressant, you know. He fell apart when he had to sell four of his stores during the pandemic."

"You think I'm losing my mind? Felicity thinks I'm totally bonkers." I let go of him and flopped back into my desk chair.

"She's only worried about you. The diamonds fiasco made her wonder if you could still run a store, so she called me. She said she can take over for a while if you need a get-away."

"What fiasco? It was Dan's job to return the diamonds to their owner, so when I discovered the 'beach rocks' were diamonds, I turned them over."

"To a man you hardly know. Have you investigated him at all?"

"Yes. I Googled him. He really is a private detective. And he has a four-star rating on Yelp."

"How many reviews?"

"One. He found somebody's French bulldog, but he lost a star for 'salty' language." I started to laugh. It was pretty funny, about the bull-dog. Kind of a low point for a detective. "Poor Dan. I suppose people who hire a detective to spy on a straying spouse don't write Yelp reviews."

Plant laughed too. "I'm taking you out to dinner. You need to put on some of your designer clothes and go out for ridiculously over-priced food and stupendous wine. We're going to that new winery restaurant on Highway Forty-One."

"Quercus? That place sounds marvelous. But I don't have that kind of money, and neither do you." I couldn't help sounding excited, although we really shouldn't spend a fortune on one night out. But even if we went somewhere else, the invitation was lovely. Just Plant and me together, like the old days. I needed some one-on-one time with him so much.

"No, but we have a gift certificate!" Plant took a strip of paper from his pocket and waved it at me. "It's for a free meal. Good for a party of four, so all we need to pay for is the wine."

"A party of four?"

"You, Felicity, Silas and me."

All I could say was, "Oh." My moment of happiness deflated. Another awkward dinner with the four of us. With Felicity dominating the conversation and me trying to disappear into the woodwork.

"It's her gift certificate, darling. It was kind of her to invite us."

"Of course it was. I'll wear my ancient Chanel suit. I think I can still fit into it." It wasn't Felicity's fault she was a difficult person, but this get-away was going to be something I'd want to get away from.

forty-two

. . .

Bruno Magli Redux

Quercus, which Felicity proudly told us all means "oak" in Latin, was a converted old ranch house snuggled into a stand of oaks on a hill overlooking the gorgeous vineyard of the Old Oak winery.

Of course, Plant, Felicity, and Silas spent the whole dinner trying to convince me I should take a vacation and leave Felicity in charge of the store. All these murders had left me frazzled, they all told me.

Frazzled. If three people thought I looked frazzled, I guess I must. Felicity said all the customers were worried about me, because I was acting so erratic and hostile. Erratic, hostile, and frazzled. Apparently that was me. A hot mess.

Silas thought I should go to New York and see my old society friends. Felicity thought I should go to Hawaii and lie on a beach, and Plant told me to go to San Diego and visit my old college friend Waverly Nelson and her husband James. Plant had been down to San Diego recently and said they had a thriving antique business and Wave was dying for me to visit.

It almost sounded tempting.

Except I didn't trust Felicity to run the bookstore by herself. Or even with an assistant — whoever that might be. She didn't even know how to count out change, for goodness' sake.

Apparently this was an intervention that had been planned in advance, so it didn't really have to do with my apparent mis-handling of the diamonds. Hey, I'd found the diamonds in the first place — didn't I get points for that? And if they all thought Dan was a phony private eye, why didn't anybody say something earlier?

All this made it difficult for me to enjoy my saffron-poached pear salad with Stilton, the lovely roasted quail with fig demi-glacé or the deliciously floral *Viognier* Plant ordered. I faked smiles and laughs as Felicity told one of her stories of meeting her schoolmate's movie star mother and staying right down the street from Oprah in Montecito. I didn't believe a word of it, but Plant and Silas ate it up.

I have to admit I felt nothing but relief when we finally got back to Morro Bay and they dropped me off at my own little home. That's all I wanted — to be in my own cozy cottage and cuddle with my kitty.

But my whole body tensed when I found the front door unlocked. Had I really done that? Left without locking my door? Maybe I really was a hot frazzled mess.

The place was dark, which is how I'd left it. And in the moonlight coming through the living room window, I could see Buckingham's little white-mustached face on the couch. But he wasn't in his usual spot. And he seemed to be sleeping on a pile of laundry. Not mine. And on the floor, I could see a pair of shoes. Expensive men's shoes.

Bruno Maglis.

Cassius Burgh?

Good Lord. Was a murderer in my house? I ran to the kitchen and grabbed the biggest knife from the drawer. I tried to take a deep breath to calm myself. I wanted to turn and run. But this man had Buckingham.

What if Dan was right and this man had killed Boyd and Orion — and maybe Bernard, too? It would mean nothing to him to bump me off. I wondered if he had that stiletto hidden somewhere on his person.

I found myself praying that Dan was a moron, and Cassius Burgh wasn't the killer Dan thought he was. But I didn't let go of the knife.

I took another breath and flicked on the living room light. I could now see the pile of laundry was a man, using two hoodies for a blanket. Yes. It really was Cassius Burgh, not quite as nattily dressed as last time.

"Camilla?" He sat up and rubbed his eyes. "Oh, thank goodness you're home. I was afraid you might not show up tonight. Sorry I fell asleep…"

He didn't sound as if he was about to stick a pointy thing in my *medulla oblongata*.

"I see you've met my cat Buckingham." I tried to sound as if my heart wasn't pounding as if it wanted to escape from my chest. The cat jumped down from his cozy spot and sauntered toward me with a reproachful meow. He didn't approve of me going out in the evening.

"Your cat is quite the gentleman." Mr. Burgh had a nice smile. "He made me feel right at home."

"And the door was, um, unlocked?" I tried to ask in a polite way if he'd broken into my house.

"No. But the key was under the geranium pot, just as Ronzo said. And you won't need that knife. I promise I have no intention of hurting you. Or your fine cat."

I put the knife back in the drawer, feeling more than a little embarrassed.

"Ronzo? You've heard from Ronzo?" Now my heart was pounding for a different reason altogether. It was too much. I plunked down in my easy chair. "Where is he? Is he here?" I had a sudden hopeful vision of him asleep in our bed, where he should be.

"No. No. he's…a prisoner, in a way. His cousins thought it would be a good idea if we hid out with their gangster buddies for a day or so while the Boyd Ferrell rumors died down out here. Man, were they wrong. Those Croatians are bad dudes. They basically kidnapped us and made us work in their warehouse for free to pay off our 'debt' to them."

I nodded. "My friend Marva, um, Marvin thought that might have happened. Have you run into Marvin Skinner? He and Ronzo were stationed in Afghanistan together."

Mr. Burgh shook his head. "I haven't seen much of anybody since I escaped two days ago. I was put in a different warehouse from

Ronzo. When they found out Ronzo had a detective license, they set him to work finding all their enemies. So they could whack them, probably." He sat up straighter on the couch. "Hey, you don't have something I could eat, do you? A bite of cheese or something? I haven't eaten since the airplane crackers on the connecting flight from Phoenix."

Oh, dear. Here was this nice, well-spoken man, a guest in my house — and I hadn't even offered him something to eat or drink. Maybe I wasn't the Manners Doctor after all.

"Of course. I have some brie and crackers. Would you like wine with that?"

"Wine?" He gave me a grin. "Oh, yes. You are so gracious. I'd love some wine."

I put together a cheese plate with the brie and some fresh grapes, then poured us both a glass from my half-finished bottle of *pinot grigio* in the fridge. Somehow the business of being a hostess calmed me down a bit. I was finally going to find out what was happening with Ronzo.

"I heard you were Orion Jones' father. I'm so sorry for your loss." I tried to sound sympathetic. "Are you here to make arrangements? Have the police released the body?"

Mr. Burgh shook his head. "I still don't know if we were related. I never did a DNA test. I guess I didn't want to know. I knew he was a hustler and a petty thief, but man, the kid could sing, and I wanted to help him. Now — I simply don't know."

"I was sorry to hear what happened. He was very talented." I desperately hoped Dan was dead wrong about Mr. Burgh. I did not want a murderer sitting in my living room.

I set the cheese plate on the coffee table, and then brought our glasses of wine. I didn't exactly need wine. There had been plenty of it at Quercus, but the buzz had worn off a bit, and now what I needed most was to get on Mr. Burgh's good side and encourage him to tell me everything he knew about my missing boyfriend.

"So you haven't seen Ronzo since you two were kidnapped?"

"I saw him some of the time. Mostly when they fed us. That's when he started telling me the stuff he was finding out about Boyd Ferrell.

He said he'd been able to sneak in some detective time of his own to try to find out what happened that night in your courtyard out there."

Buckingham had resumed his spot on the couch, and was showing a little too much interest in the cheese. I called him back to me and got him to sit on my lap, in spite of the fact I wasn't the preferred gender.

"So what did he find out? Can he prove his innocence? And yours?"

"I don't know about proof. But he had an important warning for you. That's why I'm here. He made me promise to come here immediately and tell you in person. He's worried, especially after he heard about Orion."

"So this is about Orion's murder?"

"Maybe. But it's mostly about Boyd Ferrell. It seems Boyd had a kid with a girl he met when he was on vacation in California in the late 'nineties. The woman now lives here on the Central Coast. In Atascadero, he thinks. The child's name is Francie Grimes. Or it was."

Mr. Burgh bit into a cracker that was gooey with brie. I went and got him a napkin.

"I don't think I know anybody named Francie Grimes. Does he think she was at the Moth event when Boyd died? Did she know Orion?" This was interesting information. Maybe another suspect? But I wanted to hear more about Ronzo's warning.

Mr. Burgh nodded. "I don't know if she knew Orion. But Ronzo said she did know Boyd was her father and very much resented him. Boyd ghosted her mom, who became homeless. She and Francie bounced around from one shelter to another for years. Boyd did nothing to help."

"Sounds like a terrible childhood." I was finding it hard to follow the story, but it was obvious Ronzo thought it was important I hear it.

"Apparently she managed to survive it. Francie graduated from high school in the Bay Area and went to San Jose State in the nursing program, where she got into big trouble stealing drugs. There were some mysterious deaths she was accused of as well. But she managed to get a good lawyer and only got two years in Chowchilla. But Boyd refused to help in any way."

I tried to maintain an interested smile. This was more evidence that

Boyd Ferrell had been a rotten human being. But I really needed Mr. Burgh to get to the point of the story.

"So Ronzo thinks this Francie Grimes was here on the Moth night? Is that what he wanted to warn me about? He thinks she's dangerous or something?"

"Yes. He said this young woman works for you, and she could be dangerous. Medical professionals have labeled her a sociopath. She uses the name Felicity Grant."

forty-three

. . .

Wonder Bread for Brains

r. Burgh was already awake and making coffee when I woke up. Not that I'd slept much. His bombshell revelation about Felicity had kept me tossing and turning for hours.

Felicity/Francie had been in prison, not a fancy boarding school. There were no movie star's kids or Thai princesses in her life. Her mother wasn't even dead. And Felicity was a felon. Who might possibly have killed people. But she and Silas and Plantagenet thought I had a "hostility" problem and should put her in charge of my store. I didn't know how I was going to face her today.

"Do you take milk or sugar?" Mr. Burgh offered me a cup of coffee. He did have lovely manners.

I thanked him and helped myself to the milk he'd thoughtfully put on the table. I put two English muffins in the toaster oven and motioned for him to sit at the dining table.

"I have to know something you didn't say last night." I looked him in the eye. "Does Ronzo think Felicity killed Boyd Ferrell?"

"He says it's a distinct possibility. Nobody's safe around her, he says. She's smart and vindictive. And tells outrageous lies. Gaslights people. Her last employer committed suicide. Or that's what the coroner ruled. But Ronzo has his doubts."

Dear Lord. It was as if one of those cartoon lightbulbs had turned on in my brain. All the mysterious happenings started to make sense.

"Felicity gaslights people? Do you think she might call a newspaper and plant a fake story just to sabotage somebody's business?" Scenes from the past month ran through my head like a video on fast forward. "Maybe she'd tell your neighbor you're having an affair with her godson? And post one-star reviews of your books on Amazon? And call your friends every day and tell lies about you? Try to make you think you're a hostile, frazzled hot mess?"

Buckingham meowed at my feet. My mind was so busy sorting this stuff out that I'd forgotten to feed the poor kitty.

Mr. Burgh shrugged. "You'd have to talk to Ronzo about it. He seemed to have found some reports of her behavior in an article on the death of her last employer. He was a bookstore owner in San Jose."

A bookstore owner. So she had a thing about bookstores. But she'd never learned to shelve books properly. Was that on purpose? So much of what Felicity did must have been done on purpose. Like secretly moving my coffee cup around. And claiming I wasn't the Manners Doctor. And saying I had Wonder Bread for brains. That's what the gossip columns said about me back when I was a nineteen-year-old debutante. She must have read those old articles. She probably knew everything about me — especially the parts she claimed never happened.

I buttered the English muffins and brought them to the table with some olallieberry jam. But I wasn't really hungry. I was desperate to talk to Ronzo. Right away.

"Will I ever get to see Ronzo? Will he ever get away from those people? How did you escape, anyway?"

Mr. Burgh laughed. "Those Croatians couldn't tell Black people apart. I just stole a delivery man's cap and drove his van out of there. I hope I didn't get the poor guy in trouble."

"That's not a trick that will work for Ronzo." The thought of him stuck in some warehouse doing slave labor for violent gangsters filled me with horror. "Is he going to survive this?"

"That guy made it through two tours in Afghanistan. He'll find a way. He speaks their language, so maybe he can schmooze his way out of there."

"And Marvin is there trying to help. I don't know what he can do, but he must have a plan."

"Tell me about Marvin." Mr. Burgh was making quick work of his English muffin. They must have starved him in that place. I wondered if Ronzo was starving, too.

I laughed. It was hard to tell anybody about Marvin/Marva. And knowing he was a cross-dressing dominatrix probably wouldn't give Mr. Burgh great confidence in him.

"Marvin is a master of disguise," I decided to say. "And he's pretty fearless. I don't know what his plan is, but I'm sure it will be clever."

"I hope it works. Ronzo needs to get out of there. And it seems as if you really need him here."

He'd used the word "need" twice, and he didn't seem needy or desperate. It was going to take a while for me to get Felicity's criticisms out of my head. Although, come to think of it, Mr. Burgh must be feeling pretty awful. Even if he didn't know if Orion was his real son, he obviously had some affection for him. News of Orion's death must have hit him hard after the ordeal with the Croatians.

"You didn't come to Morro Bay only to warn me about Felicity, did you? You must be here to claim Orion's body or something. Will he get a funeral?"

"I think we'll have a memorial for him at Pacific Records. He made some friends there. But the coroner is still examining the body. So I think it will be best if he's cremated after the police find out what they need to know. Lupe can keep the ashes if she wants. I haven't talked to her yet."

"Did the police tell you anything about a suspect or person of interest?"

"No. Cops are always pretty closed-mouth about suspects. But I found an important clue. One that should exonerate Ronzo."

Buckingham meowed — eager to hear about this clue too.

"That's amazingly good news," I said.

Mr. Burgh gave an odd smile. "It is. The wound that killed Orion was inflicted with a very thin instrument, like a stiletto or a hatpin. He was expertly stabbed in the back of the neck to cause almost instant death."

"Like Boyd Ferrell?"

"Exactly like Boyd Ferrell. The same person must have killed them both. And it could not have been Ronson Zolek, since he was imprisoned by gangsters in New Jersey at the time."

forty-four

· · ·

Almond Brittle

After breakfast, Cassius Burgh took his leave politely and told me to "keep my chin up" because he was sure that Ronzo would make his way home one way or another.

His opinion was probably not evidence-based, but I tried to stay positive.

But as I opened the store, I couldn't fight a looming sense of dread. I had no idea how to deal with Felicity. Or Francie, I should say. I wanted her out of my store. Out of my life. But I couldn't really fire her just because somebody told me she'd been in prison. I needed proof of some kind of wrongdoing, to protect me from a lawsuit. Mr. Burgh could have been wrong. After all, he only had second-hand knowledge of what Ronzo found in his Internet searches.

As I re-alphabetized the classic fiction section, I tried to think of the right thing to say to Felicity when she arrived at noon. I had to be polite to the woman, in spite of what I knew.

"Remember to act as if everything's normal," I told Buckingham as he settled into his favorite spot on the reading chair.

The first person to come into the store was Dan Fiedler. He didn't have any coffee with him this time. And he did buy a copy of *Sports Illustrated*. But I didn't feel as comfortable around him since Plant and

Silas and Felicity all said I'd been an idiot to give him the diamonds. It was true that he always did seem a little shady. And all his theories about Cassius Burgh being the murderer had turned out to be bogus.

He was still going on about his designated villain.

"Burgh has been spotted in Morro Bay. I hope you're keeping everything around here locked up."

I nodded. "And are the diamonds safely back with Mr. Delacorte?"

"They're safe. I'll be delivering them to my client personally in a few days. Everything peaceful around here?" Dan was leaning in a little too close.

I smiled and went back to my Ingram order. I wasn't going to tell him Mr. Burgh had spent the night in my cottage. He would probably find a reason to tell me I was an idiot to trust him. Like I was an idiot to trust Dan. Or anybody. What was I supposed to do? Wrap myself in bubble wrap and lock myself away from humans for the rest of my life?

And why hadn't Dan found out about Felicity, anyway? He didn't seem to have the sleuthing skills Ronzo had. Maybe it would be tougher to find out about her past since she'd changed her name. But she was Boyd Ferrell's daughter. That had to be a matter of record. Why hadn't Dan — or indeed, the police — looked to see if Boyd had any relatives in the area?

I should probably cut Dan some slack. After all, he was being paid to look for diamonds, not murderers.

Irene arrived with a Tarot client as Dan was leaving.

"I don't trust that man," Irene said when Dan was safely out the door. "He was always pestering Bernard. He wanted Bernard to take him out of the harbor on the *Mary Sue*. He said he used to have a yacht like her. But Bernard had spent most of the year sailing. He just wanted to rest."

All that "pestering" must have been because Dan wanted to search the yacht for the diamonds. Which of course turned out to be in my custody all along. Whether I should have given the diamonds to Dan or not, I was glad the whole surreal mess was over. But I still felt nervous when I thought how long they'd been sitting right here in my store.

And I got more jittery as the morning faded. What was I going to say to Felicity? Would I be able to pretend I didn't know she was a vicious felon who had been purposely gaslighting me? The attacks by the Freedom Patriots, the horrible Amazon reviews, the way she pretended not to believe I was the Manners Doctor — she'd done it all on purpose to make me think I was losing my mind. And it had almost worked. She got Plant and Silas to think I was bonkers, too — and urge me to take off for somewhere far away and put her in charge of the store. What would I have come home to after that vacation?

I was still angry with Plant and Silas for believing the things she said about me. Although I suppose I had been acting strange.

I usually took my lunch break when Felicity arrived at noon. But at 12:30, when she still hadn't arrived, I grabbed a protein bar from my desk to stop the stomach growls. A few minutes later, Skip rushed in and asked for her. His face scrunched up with worry as he ran his fingers through his sun-bleached hair.

"Felicity isn't here? Where is she? We can't find the candy thermometer anywhere. She didn't show up this morning to make almond brittle and now Lupe wants me to make it, but the thermometer isn't there. I don't know how to follow the recipe without a thermometer."

"The café is out of almond brittle?" A woman peeked from behind the Romance section. "Darn. I was going to buy some. My husband is addicted to the stuff." She put the book she'd been browsing back on the shelf. "I guess I'll get a cookie from Kat's across the street."

Skip looked as if he might cry.

I shook my head sadly. "I'm sorry I can't help. I haven't heard from Felicity since last night. We had dinner at Quercus with my friends Plant and Silas and they dropped her off in Atascadero around ten, and then brought me home."

"Quercus? Must be nice." Skip gave a huff. "That place costs more for one dinner than I make in a month."

"We had a gift certificate," I explained.

"A gift certificate? So that's what happened to it!" Skip gave me an accusatory look. "That was Lupe's gift certificate. She won it in a raffle last week. Damn. How did you guys get it?"

I looked around and saw several customers hovering. Encouraging

Skip's anger was unprofessional of me. But he needed to know. I lowered my voice and motioned for him to come closer to the counter.

"Felicity offered the gift certificate to Plantagenet. She didn't say where it came from. She stole it from Lupe?"

Skip nodded vigorously. "And now I guess she's stolen the candy thermometer. Or maybe she left it here? Did she leave anything here before you went to the restaurant last night?"

"She might have. How big is it? What does it look like?"

"It's actually a meat thermometer. It's red, with a digital read-out on the side. About five inches long. When it's closed, you can't really tell it's a thermometer. It looks like a long, skinny Swiss Army knife. The long, pointy needle part swings out like a switchblade."

A switchblade. With a long, pointy needle. Small enough to fit in a pocket. Puzzle pieces began to fit together in my head.

"I'll look for it when I get a chance. But I have some customers…"

He saw the two women with books waiting behind him. "Sorry. Gotta run. Maybe Felicity has showed up to the café by now."

"My son-in-law has one of those thermometers he uses when he barbecues." One woman spoke in an ominous tone as she put the latest Danielle Steel on the counter in front of me. "Lethal. They look totally lethal. I don't like him to use it around the grandkids."

Lethal indeed. More deadly than a hatpin. But long and skinny. The perfect murder weapon for somebody who'd gone to nursing school and knew how to kill with it.

Now I knew who killed Boyd Ferrel and Orion Jones. But I wondered if I could get anybody to believe me.

forty-five

. . .

Hostility

Felicity never showed up for work that day. I went over to the café after I closed the store, and asked Lupe what she knew. Lupe looked stressed. She said she was tired of telling everybody she was out of almond brittle.

The place was busy, so she didn't really have time to talk, but I thought she might tell me something about Felicity's whereabouts.

"I have no idea where that bitch is," Lupe said. "And I don't care. She's fired anyway. Skip told me what happened to my Quercus gift certificate. Maybe she got a bad oyster and died or something. One can hope."

Her voice was as icy as last time. Was I ever going to be able to get her to understand I had nothing to do with Orion or Quercus?

I took an apologetic tone. "I'm so sorry. Skip told me earlier today that she stole that gift certificate. I had no idea. She gave it to my friends Plantagenet and Silas, and we never thought to ask where she got it." I ordered a cappuccino, even though I didn't particularly want coffee.

She looked me in the eye and shook her head. "Yeah. Sorry. I know it's not your fault. She's been stealing little things from the kitchen, but I didn't want to lose her — or her almond brittle — so I didn't say anything. But then I found out she's the one who called those anti-vaxxers on me. She put my name on an anti-vax website. Right after Boyd died. Who does that?"

The milk frothing machine whished. Well, of course. That made sense. Felicity had been behind all of Lupe's woes as well as mine. I wonder if she did this awful stuff to all her employers.

I decided to take a chance, leaned in, and whispered.

"Maybe Boyd's murderer would do that? To draw attention away from herself? Did you know Felicity is a felon and an ex-con? And Boyd's daughter?"

Lupe's face went white and her hands began to shake. I had to give her points for setting down my cappuccino before she spilled it.

"Oh my god. She's the one who killed him." Lupe wasn't asking a question. She was having a revelation. Like mine. And she didn't even know about the thermometer-like wounds. Or maybe she did. "Felicity hated her father. She said so all the time. He abandoned her. That was Boyd?"

I thought back to the night of the Moth event, when I first met Felicity.

"That's one of the first things she ever said to me, too. How she wished her father was dead."

"Can we get a move-on here?" A man waiting behind me was understandably annoyed by Lupe's neglect.

"Call me, Lupe." I paid for the coffee and stood aside. "There's more."

She gave me a genuine smile. We seemed to be almost friends again. Maybe we were going to get a reset after all of this.

Back at my cottage, I fed Buckingham, foraged in the fridge for something for my dinner, and poured myself a glass of wine. In the old days, this is when I might have phoned Plantagenet, but I was still afraid Felicity's poison had soured everything with our friendship. After all, the final thing he said to me last night was that I should see a psychiatrist to deal with all my "hostility."

I was taking a first bite of a tuna melt when the phone rang. It was Plant.

"So where is she? What did you say to her? She called this afternoon saying you fired her. She's a wreck. She said she's going to be evicted and she wants to stay here. But Silas gave her a big fat no. It's been bad enough with her interrupting us with daily phone calls, but if she was living here, we'd be full time baby-sitters."

"Then why are you looking for her? Maybe she's left town."

Plant gave a deep sigh. "Because about an hour ago, when Silas and I were outside doing yard work, she left a voicemail on our landline saying she was going to off herself. I've been calling her for an hour and she doesn't pick up. Silas is on his way to her house in Atascadero. I don't suppose she's been there, has she?"

I took a sip of wine. "Slow down, Plant. Are we talking about Felicity? I didn't fire her. I haven't even seen her. She didn't show up for work today. That's all I know about her whereabouts. And by the way, she stole that gift certificate we used last night. We need to make it up to Lupe."

There was silence at the other end of the line. Then Plant spoke in a kind of choked voice. "She stole the gift certificate? But she won it in a raffle. Didn't you hear her tell that story? It was hilarious."

"Hilarious, but unfortunately entirely made up. Like everything else about her. Her real name is Francie Grimes, and she's into gaslighting people. She's been doing it to Lupe and to me. Nastiness seems to be in her genes. Maybe because she's Boyd Ferrell's daughter. I'm pretty sure she killed him."

More silence. "She…I'll have to call you back." Plant's voice went from choked to fake energetic. "Felicity! Do come in. Good to see you. We've been so worried about you! Where's Silas?"

The phone went dead.

Dear Lord. Felicity was in Plant's house in San Luis Obispo. And apparently Silas wasn't there. Plant was alone with a murderer. I wondered if she had that candy thermometer with her. Should I call the SLO police? Would they believe me when I said my employee might be planning to kill my best friend with a candy thermometer? Probably not.

While I dithered, I choked down a couple more bites of my lukewarm tuna melt. Then I heard a knock on the door. I rushed to open it, praying it would be Silas. I could tell him to rush home and save Plant.

But it wasn't Silas. It was a cheap peroxide blonde who looked as if she was trying to be Marilyn Monroe.

"I have a surprise for you, Camilla. You'll be ever so pleased." She spoke in a breathy Marilyn voice. "Here he is, bringing the luggage from the car."

And then — yes, there he was. Ronzo. With his guitar in one hand and backpack in the other. He dropped them both on the front step and bounded into the house to give me a huge hug.

"On second thought, I'll go get the luggage," Marva said.

I couldn't say anything. I had tears running down my face and couldn't let go of him. I kept touching his hair, his face, his neck. He was too thin, and his hair was scraggly and limp. But he was my Ronzo. He was home.

Buckingham started snaking around our legs. He wanted in on the hug.

Marva came back in with the luggage. "That's all. Ronzo travels light."

If I could have let go of Ronzo, I would have hugged Marva too. "You did it," I said finally. "You rescued him."

"She sure did." Ronzo finally broke from our frenzied hug. "You should have seen her flirting with those thugs. She's braver than I am."

"It helps to have a pistol in your handbag," Marva replied in her Marilyn voice. She headed for my liquor cabinet and got out the brandy bottle.

But my mind was racing. A pistol. She had a weapon. "Oh my god, Marva, I'm so glad you have a gun. We need to do something. Right away. Leave everything. This is a matter of life and death. Get back in the car. We're going to Plant and Silas's house."

"Babe, I just got home. I need a shower. And a beer. Can't this wait? Why the rush?"

"Because a gun is more threatening than a candy thermometer. Come on!" I pulled him out the door.

<h1 style="text-align: center">forty-six</h1>

. . .

<h2 style="text-align: center">It's Always Something</h2>

As Marva broke a few speed limits on the way to Plant and Silas's house, I tried to give a coherent summary of what had been happening, and why I thought Plant was in danger.

"One thing we can be sure of is that the bitch won't commit suicide," Ronzo piped up from the back seat. "That woman's rap sheet is as long as your arm, and there's no indication anywhere that she's ever suffered from depression. But she is a sociopath. I can't believe your friends were taken in by her."

"We were all taken in by her." I guess my voice sounded a little frantic. "She had me convinced I was going completely Looney Tunes."

"What about that detective guy, Dan Freidman, or something? He knew one of my cousins, so they let him talk to me on the phone. He seemed like a pretty businesslike guy. Was he taken in by Felicity, too?"

What about Dan Fiedler? Had he believed Felicity? He was the one who got me to hire her in the first place. Maybe he knew what she was doing all along.

"I don't have a clue about Dan Fiedler. Plant and Silas and Felicity think I was an idiot to trust him and give him the diamonds."

"Diamonds? You gave those uncut diamonds to some private eye?" Marva spoke with the same scornful tone I got from my dinner companions last night.

"They weren't mine. I simply wanted them out of my store." I turned around and looked at Ronzo. "I'll tell you the story later."

"Now we get to defeat your nasty little witch." Marva pulled up across from Plant and Silas's house. "I don't want to park in the driveway where she can see us. Ready, troops?"

There was only one car in the driveway — Felicity's old gray Hyundai. No sign of Silas. We could be walking into a dangerous situation.

Marva went first. She tried the door and it opened. We tiptoed into the hall and I steered them toward the living room.

"Hello, Plantagenet," Marva called out in her Marilyn voice. "You have company. Are you here?"

The living room was empty. Marva called again.

"We're in here!" Plant called from his study at the back of the house.

Plant sat at his computer desk in the corner. Felicity stood behind him. He appeared to be waiting for something to come out of his printer. He turned slowly to look at us.

"Well, hello, Ronzo! Nice to see you're back home. Camilla, good to see you. And you too, uh, Miss Monroe." He gave us all a strained smile.

"This is not Marilyn Monroe!" Felicity's high-pitched whine had a threatening tone now. "It's that drag queen Camilla thinks is so smart. Hello, Ronzo. I thought you were in jail or something. What do you guys want? We're busy here."

That's when I saw the thermometer, pointy probe out, in her right hand.

"Oh, are you helping Plant with his Netflix project?" I spoke in the overly cheerful voice I'd been using to communicate with her. "I know he's been having trouble with his co-writers. In a partnership it's always something, isn't it?"

She gave me the now-familiar look of pitying condescension.

"I don't know anything about Netflix, and I'm sure you don't either. We're printing out a lease for me to sign. I'm moving in here. They have a fantastic guest room." Felicity's smug smile made her look more demented than usual. "And Silas is the best cook. Except he serves a lot of vegetables. I don't like vegetables." She looked down at the top of Plant's head. "Tell Silas we won't be having those anymore."

"It's so great you've been helping out in the bookstore while I've been gone." Ronzo put a hand on Felicity's right shoulder.

In a flash, he had the thermometer, and Marva had her gun out of her handbag.

I took my phone from my bag and punched in 911.

Plant jumped up and he and Ronzo managed to secure Felicity's hands behind her back with some kind of computer cable while she let out a string of expletives that would have embarrassed a sailor, then collapsed into the desk chair with self-pitying moans.

I looked around. The house was strangely silent except for Felicity's wailing.

"Where's Silas?" I had a bad feeling about this. "Is he all right?"

"I'm sure he's fine. He went to Atascadero to look for Felicity…" Plant trailed off as his face mirrored my own fears. "Felicity, you didn't do anything to him, did you?"

A diabolical grin spread over her face. "You guys are such gullible idiots."

Plant grabbed his phone, hit a number, listened, then looked at me with horror. "Voice mail. I keep getting voice mail." He turned to Felicity. "I swear I'll kill you if anything's happened to him. I'll tell the police it was self-defense. Ronzo, where's that weapon of hers?"

We heard a heavy knock on the front door. The police. Thank goodness.

When Plant told them how Felicity held him hostage using a candy thermometer, the two policemen looked skeptical. But when Ronzo took the thermometer from his pocket and opened it to show the stiletto-like blade, I could see understanding dawn on their faces.

"I think you'll find that's the weapon used to kill Boyd Ferrell in Morro Bay last month, and Orion Jones last week," I said. "And she may have done something to Silas Ryder, who owns the Pierian Spring bookstore chain. He went looking for her earlier today."

Plant let out a groan and covered his face with his hands.

One of the policemen started writing furiously on his iPad. The other said he'd want to talk to us further and asked us to stop by the station later and give a statement. They put handcuffs on Felicity, returned the computer cable to Plant and marched her out the door.

We stood in silence a moment. I suppose none of us could quite process what had happened. Ronzo put an arm around me and I snuggled into his shoulder. Under all the recent drama and confusion, I felt intense relief that my man was home safe.

The front door burst open and I think I screamed, terrified Felicity had somehow escaped. But it was Silas. Plant ran to hug him.

"Call 911!" Silas said. "That lunatic woman duct-taped my wrists and ankles and shut me in a closet. Dear God, I haven't been trapped in a closet since I came out in college." He attempted a laugh. "Thank goodness her mother came home." He showed where he still had pieces of duct tape on his wrists. "She let me out and cut the tape. Poor lady. She said Felicity was 'troubled,' so she'd asked her to get help or move out. That woman is trouble all right. Has she been here?"

Plant let out a laugh that turned into a groan. He gave Silas a recap of what had just happened. Marva suggested nail polish remover to loosen the remaining duct tape.

As she went out to her car to get the polish remover, Silas plopped down on the couch and asked if we really had solved all three murders.

"So did that crazy woman kill Boyd Ferrell, Orion, and Bernard with her little thermometer? I guess I'm lucky I only got thrown in the closet. What was her motive?" Silas looked confused.

I sat in a chair across from him and tried to explain.

"She killed Boyd because he was the father who abandoned her. She'd apparently been nurturing that hate for most of her life. I'm not clear about her motives for murdering the other two — or whether she did away with all of them. It does look as if she probably killed Orion — since he got the same candy thermometer treatment. Maybe Orion figured out she'd killed Boyd. But Bernard — I don't know. He died of drowning, so it wasn't the same 'M.O.' as they call it."

"I'd like to know what that creepy Dan Fiedler had to do with all of it," Silas said. "It had to be something."

Plant laughed. "To quote Gilda Radnor, 'it's always something'." He gave Silas a hug. "Thank goodness Felicity is on her way to jail where she belongs. I hope they keep her there a long time."

forty-seven

· · ·

Goodbye Mary Sue

Okay, I admit I was late opening the store the next day. It was hard to leave the warm bed where Ronzo and I had been celebrating our reunion. Then we lingered over breakfast. He had so many hair-raising stories to tell about being kidnapped and held hostage by those gangsters.

Only one of the gangsters was actually his cousin. He was the one who had talked Ronzo and Cassius Burgh into "disappearing" when they became persons of interest. They thought they'd hide out for only a couple of days. But then they discovered they couldn't leave.

"Marko was always a little brat when he was a kid, but I never thought he'd turn out to be a soulless monster. Cassius has a friend in the FBI that he says is interested in talking to us about the gang. I hope they lock Marko and his friends up for a long time."

There were people waiting when Ronzo and I finally opened the store: Gloria, back in her raven-cape, and Irene and her Tarot client, as well as a couple of tourists.

Gloria brightened as soon as she saw Ronzo. She threw herself at him with a big bear hug, then turned to me.

"He's back! Oh, I do hope you're going to fire that horrible girl now. I heard she's a person of interest in the Boyd Ferrell murder. I'm not surprised. She was so rude. She told me to go 'F' myself when I asked her for a copy of *Go the F to Sleep*."

Felicity. I had to hope the police would keep her in custody until there was a trial. None of us would be safe with her on the loose. I'd had no idea how truly unhinged she was — or how much she hated me. Worst of all, her gaslighting had almost paid off. She and Plant and Silas had almost convinced me to let her run the store while I dealt with my "mental health issues."

But I didn't have time to think about that. At the moment I had to help the tourists find the book on Central Coast walking tours and open up the back room for Irene.

"I suppose you've heard?" Irene spoke in a stage whisper after I returned from the travel section. "The *Mary Sue*. It's gone. He sailed her out of the bay early this morning."

I froze. "What? Who? Someone took Bernard's yacht? Isn't it still a crime scene?"

"If it was, I don't think he cared." Irene gave a bitter laugh. "That man wanted Bernard's yacht from the get-go. And everything else Bernard owned. At least he gave me back the Tarot decks and crystals I left onboard. He brought them to me last night. Said those real old decks might be worth something. The Thoth deck might get five thousand dollars, he said. But he was probably lying, as usual. And he sure didn't tell me he was going to take Bernard's yacht and disappear."

"That boat never belonged to Bernard," Gloria said. "I heard about it on the news this morning. He stole it from a man named Delacorte."

"Mr. Delacorte came here to claim it?" Somehow, I'd pictured Delacorte as elderly.

"Sort of. His brother Jack took it," the Tarot client said. "Jack was here pretending to be a private eye. But he's really Mr. Delacorte's younger brother. Lupe told me about it this morning. He visited Lupe last night, too."

This Jack Delacorte must have been visiting Bernard's friends in Morro Bay while Ronzo and I were battling Felicity at Plant and Silas's house.

"He posed as a private eye?" Now Ronzo was paying attention. "Are you talking about Dan Fiedler?"

"Dan Fiedler is Jack Delacorte? The yacht owner's brother?" As I was ringing up the book on Central Coast hikes, the puzzle pieces in my brain were going click, click, click as they snapped into place. So the person I knew as "Dan" was the brother of the man Bernard had robbed of everything: his yacht, his diamonds, and even his wife. (Whom he might have killed and thrown into Avalon harbor.) "Dan" must have been pretending to be a private eye in order to get close to those of us in Bernard's circle. Especially Ronzo. He must have seriously suspected Ronzo of knowing about the diamonds because he flew all the way to New Jersey to talk to him.

And of course I was the idiot who had given Jack the diamonds, and now he had sailed off with the yacht. He'd conned me. He'd conned everybody. I wondered if he even was Eugene Delacorte's brother. Or whether there was a Eugene Delacorte.

As my brain worked on the puzzle, I smiled and wished the tourists an enjoyable hike.

Gloria nodded. "And have a nice day."

Meanwhile, I remembered "Dan" had only told me the private detective story after Bernard was dead. Before that he said he sold insurance. But he must have invented the detective story after Bernard died and there was no more hope of getting the diamonds from him. That allowed "Dan" to ask more prying questions. But how did he know Bernard was dead? They didn't find the body until three days later.

Irene had told me "Dan" kept pestering Bernard to take the *Mary Sue* out of the harbor. He said he'd owned a yacht like the *Mary Sue*. That meant he was an experienced sailor. He himself said only an experienced sailor could have taken the *Mary Sue* in and out of the harbor.

He claimed Orion must have taken the *Mary Sue*, with Bernard onboard, and killed Bernard when he wouldn't give up the diamonds — dumping his naked body at Pirate's Cove. No wonder he'd described the hypothetical murder in such detail. It was all true. Well, probably not the part about the Chinese jewel smugglers. That was pretty over the top. And also, of course, the part about Orion being a murderer.

Now I was pretty sure that even though it was Felicity who had killed Boyd and Orion, the person who had killed Bernard had to be "Dan Fiedler," AKA Jack Delacorte.

It's amazing how that man had conned us all. That Friend of the Library tee shirt had turned out to be a perfect disguise.

forty-eight

. . .

Moths to a Flame

I was kind of a zombie as I went through my day, trying to process last night's revelations about the extent of Felicity's lies and malice. How she'd been living with her mother the whole time — a mother she claimed was long dead. A mother who had thrown her out for refusing to get psychological treatment.

Luckily Ronzo got right back in the groove of working in the store, and could take over at the register. Customers loved him. I was surprised at how many people had missed him. They all told him he was so much more helpful than "that whiny girl."

Felicity had worked awfully hard to be unlikeable.

Around five-thirty, Plant phoned and asked us both to dinner. He said Silas was going to barbecue a tri-tip and was serving it with all the traditional local sides — pinquito beans, homemade salsa, and sourdough bread. It would be a welcome-home party for Ronzo.

At dinner out on Plant and Silas's patio, I was eager to tell everyone about my revelation about "Dan Fiedler"/Jack Delacorte.

"The Morro Bay police might like to hear from you," Silas said. "They had the Coast Guard arrest Delacorte this afternoon for interfering with a crime scene. The *Mary Sue* is anchored off Port San Luis now. The police have probably figured out Felicity didn't have the skills to sail her in and out of the harbor — so she couldn't have killed Bernard and thrown him overboard."

"Felicity. Damn." Plantagenet sighed. "I can't believe I was stupid enough to be taken in by such a pathetic con. And I thought it was so important to help that whiny woman. Can you forgive me, Camilla?" He reached across the table and squeezed my hand. I squeezed back. I did forgive him, but I felt some residual anger, too. It didn't make me happy that my best friend had doubted me so easily.

"It wasn't just you, Plant," Silas said. "I bought into her lies too. Not at first, but as soon as I met her in person and she did that oh-poor-me act, I wanted to help."

"Me too," I had to admit. "I found her sort of repellent, but that's why I thought I had to put up with her bad behavior and keep pretending to be her friend. To cover my feelings of guilt, I suppose. After all, I was born to privilege and she had an appalling childhood."

"Let that guilt go. As I remember your life with the countess wasn't all beer and skittles." Plant gave me a warm look that reminded me of how long we'd known each other, and what a rock he'd been for most of my life. The memory melted away some of my lingering anger.

"It's like me with my gangster cousin Marko," Ronzo said. "The truth is I never liked him. But he was so pathetic when he was a kid, because his dad had moved back to Croatia. I felt like it was my job to help him."

"It's because we're empathetic people," Plant said. "People with empathy always want to be Good Samaritans. We want to make things better. Maybe that's arrogant of us. At least it makes us perfect targets for the sociopaths who use self-pity as a weapon.

I nodded as I watched the moths flying way too close to the fire in the barbecue grill. "We're like those pathetic little moths, attracted to the flame that's going to kill them."

"Did you know it turns out moths are not actually attracted to flame or other man-made light sources?" Silas was in his bookish "little known facts" mode. "It's because the light disorients them. It discombobulates their navigation system and they lose sight of where they're going."

I laughed. "So we're not actually attracted to the bad guys. They just discombobulate us?"

"That's about the size of it." Ronzo lifted his glass. "Here's to not letting them discombobulate our moths next time."

"May our future moths remember where they're going — and what's really important." I put down my glass and leaned over to give Ronzo a kiss.

about the author

Anne R. Allen is a popular blogger and the author of the hilarious Camilla Randall Mysteries as well as the comic novels *Food of Love, The Gatsby Game,* and *The Lady of the Lakewood Diner.* Her nonfiction book, *The Author Blog: Easy Blogging for Busy Authors,* is an Amazon #1 best-seller. She's also the co-author, with Catherine Ryan Hyde, of the writer's guide *How to Be a Writer in the E-Age.*

Anne is a graduate of Bryn Mawr College and now lives on the Central Coast of California near San Luis Obispo, the town Oprah called "the happiest town in America."

Anne loves to hear from her readers. Contact her at annerallen.allen@gmail.com. You can also follow her at her Amazon page and at BlueSky and Facebook

She blogs with *NYT* million-copy seller, Ruth Harris, at "Anne R. Allen's Blog…with Ruth Harris." You can find them at annerallen.com. The blog was named one of the Best 101 Websites for Writers by *Writer's Digest.*

If you've enjoyed this book, we hope you will consider writing a brief review. It will help others find the book. Thanks!

books by anne r. allen

THE CAMILLA RANDALL MYSTERIES: Chick Lit Noir— Snarky, delicious fun! These books are a laugh-out-loud mashup of romantic comedy, crime fiction, and satire. Dorothy Parker meets Dorothy L. Sayers. Perennially down-and-out socialite Camilla Randall--a.k.a. "The Manners Doctor"--is a magnet for murder, mayhem and Mr. Wrong, but she always solves the mystery in her quirky, but oh-so-polite way. Usually with more than a little help from her gay best friend, Plantagenet Smith.

#1 GHOSTWRITERS IN THE SKY: After her celebrity ex-husband's ironic joke about her "kinky sex habits" is misquoted in a tabloid, New York etiquette columnist Camilla Randall's life unravels in bad late night TV jokes. Nearly broke and down to her last Hermes scarf, she accepts an invitation to a Z-list Writers' Conference in the wine-and-cowboy town of Santa Ynez, California, where, unfortunately, a cross-dressing dominatrix named Marva plies her trade by impersonating Camilla. When a ghostwriter's plot to blackmail celebrities with faked evidence leads to murder, Camilla must team up with Marva to stop the killer from striking again.

#2 SHERWOOD, LTD: Suddenly-homeless American manners expert Camilla Randall becomes a 21st century Maid Marian—living rough near the real Sherwood Forest with a band of outlaw English erotica publishers—led by a charming, self-styled Robin Hood who unfortunately may intend to kill her.

#3 THE BEST REVENGE (the prequel): Read how it all began. In the glitzy 1980s, a teenaged Camilla loses everything: fortune, love, and eventually even her freedom when a TV star's murder is mistakenly laid at her feet. Through it all, she perseveres, and comes to learn that she is made of sterner stuff than anyone might have imagined, herself included.

#4 NO PLACE LIKE HOME: Doria Windsor, the uber-rich editor
of *Home* decorating magazine loses everything, including her Ponzi-schemer
husband, when their luxury wine-country home mysteriously goes up in
flames. Homeless, destitute, presumed dead and branded a criminal, 59-yr-old
Doria has a crash course in reality…and a second chance at love.

Meanwhile, Camilla Randall is facing homelessness, too, as Doria's husband's
schemes unravel and take down innocent bystanders along the way. When the
mysterious—and dangerously attractive—Mr. X. turns up at Camilla's
bookstore looking for clues to the death of a missing homeless man, Camilla
joins in the search.

With the help of brave trio of homeless people and a little dog named Toto,
Doria, Camilla and Mr. X journey down their own yellow brick road to
unmask the real killer and reveal the dark secrets of Doria's "financial wizard"
husband.

#5 SO MUCH FOR BUCKINGHAM: Camilla makes the mistake of
responding to an Amazon review of one of her etiquette guides and sets off a
chain of events that leads to arson, attempted rape and murder. Her best friend
Plantagenet Smith is accused of the murder and nobody but her shady former
boyfriend Peter Sherwood—fresh from a Tasmanian prison—can save him.

Camilla and Plant are caught between rival factions of historical reenactors
who are fiercely pro or anti-Richard III. Set against the backdrop of Richard's
re-burial in Leicester in 2015, the book is an exploration of the power of false
rumors as well as a satire of the Internet communities whose "flame wars"
sometimes spill into real life.

#6 THE QUEEN OF STAVES: Camilla's boyfriend Ronzo is forced to stage his
own death and hide out in a homeless camp after his review angers a
homicidal rock band. But he's able to help Camilla keep her struggling Morro
Bay bookstore afloat with his unexpected tarot reading skills…until the lover
of one of his tarot clients turns up dead on the beach. It's up to Camilla and
Ronzo — and the tarot cards — to solve the mystery. Meanwhile, Camilla's ex-
husband Jonathan Kahn resurfaces, sparking old feelings, and Ronzo has a
new rival: a too-perfect doctor who may or may not be in cahoots with a gang
of murderous New-Agers who believe Camilla knows the whereabouts of the
legendary lost Braganza emeralds.

#7 GOOGLING OLD BOYFRIENDS: Camilla befriends socialite Mickie
McCormack, who's going through a painful divorce. Mickie has been Googling
her old boyfriends in order to reconnect and "remember who she used to be."
Unfortunately, every one of those boyfriends soon ends up dead. Is the serial

killer Camilla's old boyfriend Dr. Bob? Or another one of Mickie's old boyfriends? And can Camilla's old boyfriend Captain Rick Zukowski of the L.A.P.D. protect her and her cat Buckingham from being fed to the sharks before she solves the mystery?

#8 CATFISHING IN AMERICA: At her beach-read bookstore in Morro Bay California, everybody tells Camilla their troubles. When the body of talkative widow Ginny Gilhooly shows up on Camilla's doorstep, Camilla is sure the online scammer who has been "catfishing" Ginny has murdered her. But Ginny's body disappears, and Camilla's unhoused friend "Hobo Joe" is accused of the murder. Camilla, with the help of two precocious Nancy Drew wannabes, and her cat Buckingham, must solve the mystery of the travelling corpse and prove Joe had nothing to do with Ginny's demise.

These **three comic novels** are available in the boxed set,

BOOMER WOMEN: THREE COMEDIES ABOUT A GENERATION THAT CHANGED THE WORLD

FOOD OF LOVE (Romantic-comedy / thriller) After Princess Regina, a former supermodel, is ridiculed in the tabloids for gaining weight, someone tries to kill her. She suspects her royal husband wants to be rid of her, now she's no longer model-thin. As she flees the mysterious assassin, she discovers the world thinks she is dead, and seeks refuge with the only person she can trust: her long-estranged foster sister, Rev. Cady Stanton, a right-wing talk show host who has romantic and weight issues of her own. Cady delves into Regina's past and discovers Regina's long-lost love, as well as dark secrets that connect them all.

THE GATSBY GAME (Romantic-comedy / mystery):

When Fitzgerald-quoting con man Alistair Milborne is found dead in a movie star's motel room—igniting a world-wide scandal—the small-town police can't decide if it's an accident, suicide, or foul play. As evidence of murder emerges, Nicky Conway, the smart-mouthed nanny, becomes the prime suspect. She's the only one who knows what happened. But she also knows nobody will ever believe her. The story is based on the real mystery surrounding the death of David Whiting, actress Sarah Miles' business manager, during the filming of the 1973 Burt Reynolds movie *The Man Who Loved Cat Dancing.*

THE LADY OF THE LAKEWOOD DINER (Romantic-comedy/mystery)

Someone has shot aging bad-girl rocker Morgan le Fay and threatens to finish the job. Is it fans of her legendary dead rock-god husband, Merlin? Or is the secret buried in her childhood hometown of Avalon, Maine? Morgan's childhood best friend Dodie, the no-nonsense owner of a dilapidated diner, may be the only one who knows the dark secret that can save Morgan's life. And both women may find that love really is better the second time around. Echoes of the Grail legend bring into focus the nature of nostalgia and the pitfalls of longing for a Golden Age that never was.

WHY GRANDMA BOUGHT THAT CAR: A collection of short stories and verses—humorous portraits of rebellious women at various stages of their lives. From aging Betty Jo, who feels so invisible she contemplates robbing a bank, to neglected 10-year-old Maude, who turns to a fantasy Elvis for the love she's denied by her patrician family, to a bloodthirsty Valley Girl version of Madam Defarge, these women—young and old—are all rebelling against the stereotypes and traditional roles that hold them back. Which is, of course, why Grandma bought that car…

Nonfiction by Anne R. Allen

HOW TO BE A WRITER IN THE E-AGE: A SELF-HELP GUIDE co-written with Amazon superstar Catherine Ryan Hyde. This guide offers warm, friendly advice on how to start and sustain a writing career. You'll see a lot of books out there about how to write, and a whole lot more that promise ebook millions. But this book is different. It helps you establish a professional writing career in this time of rapid change—and answers the questions so many writers are asking: Does an author still need an agent? Can new writers still get published by Big Five publishers? What about digital-only imprints, mid-sized publishers, small presses—or should everybody self-publish? Do you need to spend endless hours on social media? How do you cope with rejection, depression, bad reviews and other downsides of the writing profession? Anne and Catherine answer all these questions and more in this fun, information-packed book.

THE AUTHOR BLOG: EASY BLOGGING FOR BUSY AUTHORS Named one of the "Best Blogging Books of All Time" and "Best SEO Books of All Time" by Book Authority. Anne's easy-does-it guide to simple, low-tech blogging for authors who want to build a platform, but not let it take over their lives. She'll tell you why an author blog doesn't have to follow all the rules that monetized business blogs do. You'll learn the secrets that made Anne a multi-award-winning blogger and one of the top author-bloggers in the business—and why having a successful author blog is easier than you think.

www.ingramcontent.com/pod-product-compliance
Lightning Source LLC
Chambersburg PA
CBHW070420310726
48977CB00003B/768